Word Storms

Also by SpearPoint Publications

Snapshots: Flash Stories from Random Lives
By Howard Schneider, with Mizeta Moon

Aliens, Fish Tales & Flying Hooves
By Mizeta Moon

Monkey Casserole: 33 Selected Short Stories
By Howard Schneider, Mizeta Moon & Linda Burk

Embracing Evil
By Mizeta Moon

Word Storms

Original Fiction

by

Mizeta Moon

Howard Schneider

Silver Gladstar

SpearPoint Publications
Portland, Oregon

Copyright © 2017 by F. Howard Schneider, Redwood La Chapel and Silver Gladstar

All rights reserved under International and Pan-American Copyright Conventions.

Published in the United States by SpearPoint Publications, Portland, OR
2017

Cover created by Zap Graphics, Portland, Oregon

To Ryan
& Family
Love from
Mizeta

To Ryan!
Thank you!
Woohoo!
-Siher

Ryan
Happy reading!
Howard

♡ Mom

Table of Contents

Preface IX
Portraits of Carrolltown — *Mizeta Moon* 1
Workers Unite — *Howard Schneider* 58
Hello Seniors — *Howard Schneider* 63
Archie — *Mizeta Moon* 66
Just Stories — *Howard Schneider* 69
Now Where Is She — *Howard Schneider* 72
Dinner at the Top of the World — *Mizeta Moon* 74
Santa's Beer Sleigh — *Mizeta Moon* 77
Reading in the Park — *Howard Schneider* 79
Eager to Serve/The Zealous Juror — *Mizeta Moon* 81
It's About Norman Ziglinski — *Howard Schneider* 83
Deaf Bartender — *Mizeta Moon* 87
The Horror — *Howard Schneider* 95
A Blue Ribbon — *Howard Schneider* 98
Autopsy — *Mizeta Moon* 103
When Too Much Is Enough — *Howard Schneider* 106
Recall — *Mizeta Moon* 111
Busking — *Howard Schneider* 113
Wheelchair Power — *Howard Schneider* 117
Raucous Offerings — *Silver Gladstar* 167

Preface

Dear Reader,

Portraits of Carrolltown is a story told in 29 individually titled vignettes, averaging one-half to three pages. This story is best read in one sitting, in order to absorb the emotional thread tying them together.
We have also included some of the recent flash stories for which we are known, and wrap up our excursion into the bizarre and unusual with Wheelchair Power, an eight-part adventure featuring an unlikely hero and lots of twists and turns.
There is also a bonus story by a previously unpublished author that we believe has a unique voice begging to be heard.
Thank you for your purchase, and we hope you enjoy our
latest offering.

SpearPoint Publications

Portraits of Carrolltown
By Mizeta Moon

Part One
Plowman

"I'm a plowman," the weather-ravaged man with a heavily lined face and yellowed teeth said, when I asked him to describe himself.

"I spend my days in hot sun, furrowing ground that often resists my thrusts. Meeting such resistance, I am required to lean heavily on the handles and drive my blade deep into the soil to accomplish the desired result. Is it any wonder that my mule and I are much the same? Our stubbornness and unyielding personalities are what the job mandates. Weakness is not within our lexicon, and rest is what comes only at the end of the day."

I was overwhelmed by his resolve and preacher-like eloquence. I'd been photographing rural America while developing material for my next gallery showing, and rolled into Carrolltown expecting the usual mix of humanity. Carrolltown was a flyspeck on my map that turned out to be a time-capsule farming village, nestled in a lush pocket valley beneath granite cliffs topped by towering conifers. I wasn't prepared to meet a man so deep, who was filled with a potency that could only be drawn from intimate communion with nature. The essence of the earth upon which we tread radiated from his every pore.

While we sat on coarse wooden benches on the porch of a ramshackle home, I studied his iron-gray hair and sinewy sun-bronzed arms. His fingers were a tapestry of scars and blunted nails. His dingy white shirt had been patched many times, and his jeans were threadbare and worn, but there was dignity in every remaining thread. He'd earned every callus, bruise and cut by slogging through wind, rain and drought to provide his neighbors with an opportunity to plant seed. How could I not desire a portrait of such a man?

"Farmers around here call me Plowman, but my name is Harlan if you want to write that on the back of the picture," he said shyly. His humility was intoxicating in its sincerity. In his company I felt ashamed of my arrogance.

I looked down at his boots that needed new heels and were held together by laces that had been broken and retied many times. I felt like crying as I imagined how little he might have to eat and what a pitiful mattress he must lie on at night. My suite at a motel thirty miles away, with its perfumed soaps and chocolates on the pillow, seemed far removed at the moment. I was nothing, in all my fame, when compared to such an enormous soul. I had finally found a portrait of a man. Could I capture it with my lens? It was a challenging question only time could answer.

"Do you need me to smile?" he asked. "I smile a lot when I'm working. The birds and I sing together all the time. Sadie, my mule, doesn't like birds much, but I pay her no mind, because birds need the worms turned up by my plow. Sadie gets a half-bale of hay every night and the spring runs deep and cold beside her corral. She works hard for me and regularly complains, but she secretly enjoys it, even though she acts like an idiot sometimes. Oh … am I talking too much? Ma was always saying I had a loose tongue."

While his brilliant blue eyes looked at me intently, I snapped the shutter, having found the pose I wanted. A man. Questioning the future, past and present at once, without uttering a word.

"Have I done well?"
"Did you get what you wanted?"
"What else should I do?"
As I asked myself the same questions.

The Plowman's Wife

It had been so quiet inside the house that I was startled when a woman opened the screen door and politely asked us to come in for a glass of iced tea. Introductions were made, and at first I hesitated to accept, not wanting to tax their resources. At Sarah's insistence, I stepped into a room that destroyed all of my preconceptions.

The floor was hard-packed dirt, swept smooth by a straw broom that rested near a hearth made of the same granite I'd seen permeating the area. Instead of a meager cot, a sturdy hand-hewn bed was covered by a rag quilt that must have taken weeks to sew. On a plank table, sliced from the heart of a giant oak, stood a kerosene lantern, which seemed to be the only source of lighting in the room. Upon it sat two pairs of reading glasses, along with a Webster's dictionary, the Farmer's Almanac and an encyclopedia. I immediately understood Harlan's eloquence. I envisioned the two of them, sitting for hours in flickering light, reading to each other and sharing precious moments my generation had yet to embrace. There were only two ladder back chairs. Sarah stood while Harlan and I sat.

Sarah was barefoot, with splayed toes peeking out from under an ankle-length gingham dress that had been washed so many times its colors were faded. Her once coal-black hair was now streaked with silver, but her ramrod-straight posture and still-supple skin belied her age. Her chapped hands told Sarah's story. She explained to me, as we sipped our tea from jelly jars, that she was a laundress who took in washing from families overburdened by chores and children, and constant demands for their time as they eked out a living from the land. By listening to her, I came to understand that the fertile land of the valley residents now farmed was originally overlaid by layers of rock that had to be wrestled from the ground by men and mules. The exposed soil underneath had then been coaxed into usability by Harlan's plow, along with those of many generations before theirs.

As we talked, I stood and began to wander about the room. Looking out the back window, I saw sheets hanging on a cotton rope line that was supported by galvanized iron posts. Everything she'd laundered was held in place by wooden clothespins. Children's clothes and men's overalls were drying in a gentle breeze blowing across a neatly trimmed yard bordered by flowerbeds. A vegetable garden further back was filled with plants that looked ready to surrender their bounty. Giant sunflowers awaiting harvest tilted heads heavily laden with seeds. There was a row of cages near a tumble-down wooden fence, and I saw what appeared to be animals inside them. When I inquired as to their contents, Sarah told me they raised rabbits for meat because coyotes and foxes preyed on chickens left free to roam. When they needed eggs, she bartered homemade jelly or rabbit meat with farmers who could afford large barns filled with fowl.

The anomaly in the room was two silver picture frames on the mantel. They held smiling portraits of what appeared to be the same young man in two different suits. When I neared them, Sarah swelled with pride and spoke with tenderness only a mother could convey.

"Those are my boys. Twins, born right here in that bed. Everything we earn that isn't needed to keep us alive goes to their education. They go to City College, over in Lewisburg. Caleb, the one on the right, wants to be a doctor and open a practice here in Carrolltown. His brother John is majoring in agricultural science so he can help local farmers get greater yields from their crops. He also feels they need to develop greater diversity in their planting."

It was then that I snapped her picture. Her pride, and utter joy at having her sacrifices yield such a reward, filled my lens with a glow I cannot describe with mere words. I no longer pitied the two of them. I felt honored to have made their acquaintance.

Carrolltown

I was experiencing an epiphany and knew it. I was suddenly seeing everything in a different light. The world around me gained greater substance and texture as I drove into the center of town. There were only nine hundred residents, and the town wasn't much more than a crossroads, but I now understood that this hub was a cohesive force, holding together lives of importance.

I pondered repetition and perseverance as I viewed a schoolhouse that required thousands of granite blocks to be quarried, cut to size, and then placed in their current positions. Hour after hour. So much toil. Aches and pains a caustic reward for trying to better their lot in life. Why? I asked myself. Why does mankind struggle so hard to live, when only death waits at the end?

Every building harkened to the nineteenth century, even if they were of recent construction. There were a few cars and pickups parked on well-maintained streets, but horses, mules, buggies and wagons outnumbered them. Most of the men dressed in jeans or overalls. The women dressed conservatively, but didn't appear to be bound by religious tenets. If anything, they looked like women who worked hard and had no need for fashion they could ill afford. I pulled up next to the bank and parked. Getting out and stretching, I wrapped my camera's tether around my arm and went for a stroll.

Carrolltown was founded by Flavius Carroll. The first white settler to travel this far west, he claimed the valley and was granted its title by presidential decree. He'd served honorably in the army and was thus rewarded for his loyalty and bravery. I learned all this from a bronze plaque mounted on a granite boulder beneath a maple tree so big it had to have been there for a hundred years or more. I assumed there'd been no sculptor in town after he died. Anyway, the town has his name on it.

I was hungry, so I looked around for a diner. A sign on the front of a livery-stable-like building said **Grub**. Hoping that meant hot soup and a salad, I crossed the street and discovered the subject of my next portrait.

You may think I'm referring to the waitress in hot pants and tank top, but you'd be wrong. She was the owner's granddaughter, and one of the few rebellious youth in town. Maybe the cook?

He was a sloppy mess in a wife beater T-shirt and sporting a two day beard. I'd obviously stepped forward in time. Starving, I decided to risk it and sat in a corner booth. After the young lady had taken my order, I glanced around the room.

The walls were papered with rodeo posters. Several photos of a bronco rider in action were prominently placed. Looking closely, I saw a resemblance between the man on the horses and the guy who was mangling my salad and scalding my soup in a microwave oven.

Two couples sat in booths, eating and flirting with their eyes, possibly dreaming about what might transpire.

An elderly woman hunched over a plate of meatloaf and mashed potatoes as if someone might rob her of it.

The only black man I'd seen so far was scribbling furiously with a pencil on an overly large pad of paper.

The subject of my next portrait sat in the corner opposite me. He was nearly invisible because of his diminutive stature. If he had not dropped his fork and bent to retrieve it, I might never have noticed him. Abandoning the food that had been both poorly prepared and served, I stood and approached his table. Was I always this bold? I asked myself, as I closed the gap between us.

Quarryman

When I'd introduced myself to the man in the corner booth the evening before and shook his oversized hand, it was like gripping a fence post wrapped with sandpaper. His musclebound forearms and bulging biceps seemed disproportionate to his height until I took stock of his stump-like torso. He was perfect for his profession. The shortness of his legs provided leverage a taller man would have lacked. With no need to stoop, he could move blocks of granite by lifting them over his head with ease. He reminded me of Atlas, carrying the weight of the world on his mighty shoulders.

We'd agreed to meet this morning at the quarry, located on a gravel road outside the Carrolltown city limits. When I parked next to a manufactured home that obviously served as office and residence to the quarryman, I noticed that it had white curtains behind clean windows, and a plethora of plants grew in containers lining a walkway composed of packed granite pebbles. My stereotypes no longer held to form, as I'd expected a dust-choked industrial site. Looking up, I saw a satellite dish on the roof, which seemed out of character with the rest of Carrolltown. No car was in sight.

I gathered my camera and water bottle, then started towards the office, but before I reached it, a three-wheel ATV roared up and came to a sliding stop in front of me.

"Good morning. Glad you could make it. Ready to take pictures?"

Although his smile was welcoming, I detected a hint of reservation in the set of his shoulders. Was he worried that I might portray him in a bad light, or demean him somehow? Ignoring these signals, I greeted him warmly, then climbed onto the ATV.

"Ready," I said, "but please take it easy. This is my first time on one of these things."

Several minutes later, we sat looking into the largest pit I'd ever seen. It was obvious that centuries of toil had been required to excavate such a monstrous hole. Men using picks and shovels hundreds of feet below looked like ants. Mule-driven wagons waiting to ferry blocks of granite seemed to me like something out of an old-time movie. To witness such industriousness filled me with appreciation of the sheer brutality required to harvest granite and transform it into architectural works of art.

"Want to go down? Or would you rather stay up here? I'm not sure what you meant when you said you wanted a portrait of me."

"What do you do all day?" I asked. "Do you dig? Supervise? Sit in the office? I can tell you've paid dues down there, but are you simply a boss now? No insult intended, but this machine we're on seems out of place with everything else I see. Honestly, I expected lots of machinery and dozens of trucks, but with that not being the case, I'm a little confused."

"That's understandable," he said earnestly. "There's just so much to do these days that I tire out my horses and mules, or they become footsore from stepping on shards. The ATV can get to the bottom quickly, and also whisk me into town if we need something. The demand for countertops alone keeps us busy from dawn to dusk."

Before I could interrupt, he continued.

"I know what you're thinking. Why not use machinery? Why not make it easier?"

I remained silent through his pause, understanding that a portion of his soul was about to be revealed.

"Tradition. It's that simple. We are hard men, but we love our wives and children. We love the homes we build with our own hands. What we do here adds to the wellbeing of our entire community. We come to work each day with determination and anticipation, not reluctance. This land is our provider, but it begs a heavy toll of us to claim its bounty."

"Our mules are our brethren. We share our corn with them, and the water that flows through our valley. Without them, we would be forced to be what you expected."

"Every man has his favorite tool, and we work as one to bring our product to market. I myself have worked every job and have filled in many times where needed. My great-great grandfather started excavations here soon after Carrolltown was founded. I've modernized my personal life a bit, but every slab, block or stone that leaves here will be quarried by hand."

It was then that I captured the bead of sweat sliding down his brow with my lens; the absolute determination in his eyes that had attracted me from the start; the jawline above a corded neck that radiated strength.

I framed him against a cliff. Sunlight highlighted his tawny hair. His power was absolute. He was a master of stone.

No Rose-Colored Glasses

I wouldn't want to be accused of romanticizing things. Heaven forbid there be something special in a jaded world. I found the drug house right away. Heard talk in the coffee shop about how the sheriff had had enough of such shenanigans and was about to come down hard. I saw the town drunk staggering home from the bar, leaning against a streetlight to vomit his excess. But, to tell the truth, I was in love with the idea of hard work and focused my attention elsewhere. Most of these people were putting their nose to the grindstone to ensure their survival.

Fingers probing deep in the soil to sow. Towing a burgeoning burlap sack while harvesting. Weeding with a hoe instead of employing a tractor. I was impressed and wanted to know more. Towards that end, I inquired about rooms to rent so I could stay for a while and leave the world of motels and freeway ramps behind.

As luck would have it, Marlene Squires' house was available. Her husband had recently died and she was heading off to Europe with the insurance money. Minimal rent. Mow the lawn. Pay the light bill, etc. I moved in the next day as Marlene raised a cloud of dust with her departure.

The Welcome Wagon

There wasn't a doorbell. There was a buzzer that went **bzzt, bzzt, bzzt.** I had been sleeping soundly and resented any intrusion on my dreams.

Tiredly, I made my way to the door, where I was greeted by an overload of cheerfulness. Evidently, I was new, and tradition required that I be greeted in the appropriate manner, even if it was seven-thirty in the morning. I smiled my way through introductions, even though I remembered no names. You have to keep in mind that I hadn't had coffee or a chance to pee.

Having accepted more cakes, cookies and casseroles than I could eat in a month, I finally eased a gaggle of well-meaning women out the door. Rushing to the bathroom, I barely made it in time. Feeling there was no point in going back to bed, I stepped into the shower, thinking about my next portrait.

Fisherman

It was a beautiful day, so I decided to go for a walk. I felt the sound of my car would be an intrusion when juxtaposed to creaking harnesses and clopping hooves. Besides, nothing in Carrolltown was very far away. Camera in hand, I followed a dirt path beside the river Carrolltown hugged the banks of, hoping for something wonderful to document.

The path led into a copse of trees that formed a canopy, allowing only filtered light to reach leaf-strewn ground beneath them. I was disappointed at first, having done my share of nature photography, and moved on. The sound of water surging over rocks caught my attention, however, and I forged ahead, expecting rapids.

What I found instead was a waterfall that plunged from a granite shelf some thirty feet above a large pool. The pool emptied over a ledge, then the water raced past a series of giant boulders. I suspected that children had swum in the pool for ages. The canopy of trees gave way to a clearing where the night sky would showcase its millions of stars. It was an idyllic setting for romance or communing with the universe. As I listened more closely, birdcalls echoed over the roar of water. Looking up to find their source, I noticed a wooden bridge that spanned the waterfall and clung to the shoulders of two hills.

The path started to climb after passing the pool, so I continued upwards, consumed by curiosity about what lay beyond. After traversing several switchbacks that reduced the gradient, I arrived at the bridge. Iron spikes driven into the granite anchored cables wrapped around stone stanchions thicker than my torso. They had obviously been hewn by hand. The span extended across the river and merged with a similar mounting on the other side. Everything appeared in good repair, so after looking at the spectacular view for a few moments, I crossed without trepidation.

The path continued, but now wandered through a flower-laden meadow that buzzed with sounds of bees. Several man-made hives stood in brilliant sunshine, beckoning the winged gatherers to store their bounty within. In the distance, a herd of cows bowed their heads to graze from grass that was knee-deep and rife with floral scents. I felt transported into a magical land where time stood still, and tawdriness from the outside world had yet to stain its tranquility.

Rounding a bend, I encountered a wide spot in the river where the water was shallow and pebbles were clearly visible beneath it. An ancient oak spread its massive branches to the sky, while its exposed upper root structure claimed the bank like a nobleman who'd been granted entitlement no one could rescind. It was in a swirling eddy that I spied the subject of my next portrait.

Wearing hip-waders, a khaki shirt, and a floppy green canvas hat that was peppered with fishing lures, he stood quietly mid-stream, casting up-river and watching patiently while his brilliantly colored fly floated past him. When it reached the end of his line, he would reel it back, then cast again. Not wishing to disturb him, I watched from afar, relishing the simplicity of his joy. There was no tension in his body language. No burning desire to catch something, or else. He was one with the elements, and their embrace was his reward. I captured him at the release point, where nearly invisible line cleaved the air and delivered his fly to swiftly flowing water. Afterwards, I quietly turned away and retraced my steps.

A Visitor

The house I'd rented was comfortable. Fairly up-to-date plumbing, with a deep and wide tub for soaking. A kitchen with a gas stove from another era, but perfectly functional when it came to making breakfast. Electric lighting and a television, although reception was poor, using rabbit ears wrapped in aluminum foil. I'd learned through local gossip that cable networks were not interested in laying fiber-optics due to a lack of subscribers, and that the few modernists were reliant on satellite dishes. Evidently, Marlene had other uses for her money.

I'd been contemplating a trip to the butcher shop to try my hand at pot roast, when the buzzer interrupted with its obnoxious sound.

At the door stood a lanky man dressed in overalls, wearing a wide-brimmed straw hat that had seen better days. He obviously didn't own a razor, as his beard sprouted in every direction and went nearly to his waist. His eyes were piercing, although his voice and mannerisms were soft when he spoke.

"May I help you?" I asked, hoping he wasn't selling anything.

"I've come to repair the fence," he replied. "Marlene asked me to stop by last week, but my cow was calving and I didn't have time. She said you probably wouldn't mind that I was here."

"That's fine," I replied. "Did she pay you? Or am I supposed to?"

"Everything is taken care of," he said. "Except for a couple boards I need that she said would be in the shed. I looked, but she must have forgot. I probably don't have to tell you that she was in a big hurry to leave. I can charge them at the lumberyard if you like."

Observing his awkwardness at asking a stranger for money, I was once again reminded of the synergy between neighbors and friends that relied on trust and was perpetuated by integrity. I asked him how much he needed, then retrieved the insignificant amount from my billfold.

"Thank you," he said humbly. "I'll try not to make too much noise."

I should have invited him in, but was still too citified in my ways to trust callers at the door. Later in the day I would offer him lemonade, only to find he'd brought a water bottle, some cornbread and a can of pork and beans. That evening, the pot roast sat woodenly in my mouth when I contemplated the work ethic of these people who wanted nothing but to live peacefully in their valley and partake of nothing they had not earned by the sweat of their brow. What had I to offer to such folk? My pictures hung in galleries throughout the world, but were worthless in a blizzard, as they would provide little warmth when burned. They meant nothing to a person who worked from sunrise to sundown to feed a family. I began to wonder if I had ever truly added anything to the world. I barely knew how to start a fire, let alone fell a tree and build shelter. In darkness, cold and deprivation, could I be counted on to do more than provide aesthetics when bellies hungered and wolves clamored at the door?

Moonlight

I was restless. Sounds of wind blowing outside a strange house were keeping me awake. Unfamiliar creaks led to flights of imagination, and a loose shutter rattling became an irritant I would not have noticed amid the noise of a city. At such times back home, I would have driven to an all-night market and bought ice cream or walked to the corner bar for a nightcap and some company. Carrolltown rolled up its sidewalks after dark and the tavern closed at midnight. The general mercantile was open only from dawn to dusk, which meant there was no ice cream available unless I drove to Lewisburg, twenty-five miles away down a stretch of dark winding highway.

Realizing sleep was a futile pursuit, I padded barefoot into the kitchen, thinking a cup of chamomile tea might soothe my jangled nerves. Waiting for water to boil, I noticed shadowy patterns of waving branches sliding back and forth across the semi-opaque window of a door leading to the back yard. I knew the outer light was not on, as I could see the switch plate, and certainly there was no streetlight that could be illuminating the house, as it sat by itself on a hill well away from Main Street. I poured water over a teabag, then cradling the warmth of my favorite cup, I unlocked the door, wondering where such strong light could be coming from.

Descending three wooden steps leading to the yard, I stepped into a fairyland bathed in moonlight. An enormous full moon hung like a beacon over a ridge laden with trees. It nearly blotted out the blackness upon which it rested, but a blanket of stars quietly shone outside the moon's halo. Carrolltown was bathed in a wash that created a black and white etching defined by tones of gray. A church steeple rose above the sleeping village, where no movement could be discerned. Empty streets were but lines defined by black shadows. The graveyard seemed eerie in such quietude, and every building was dark, save three lighted windows. It was as if I alone existed on this windswept hill. Suddenly aware that the wind had quickened, I pulled my robe closer as I ventured further.

Noticing movement, I looked up to see a family of deer walking slowly into underbrush bordering Marlene's unattended vegetable garden. I'd already had thoughts of resurrecting it in her absence. They disappeared, and it was then I realized that I wasn't alone. A German shepherd sat looking at me with eyes that shone with curiosity. I sensed immediately that the dog posed no threat, and merely wondered where it had come from. Speaking softly, I asked it to join me.

We sat for hours watching the night unfold. A few clouds passed by, but did nothing to dim the wonder we shared. Had we been able to converse, it would have been both unnecessary and intrusive. Eventually, morning dew began to settle on the grass, turning its blades silvery and reminding me of winter. A band of rose-colored light began to tint the eastern sky, and that magnificent moon finally slipped below the ridge. Sensing that it was time to part ways, the dog stood, shook itself, then trotted away without a sound. I shivered, realizing I was wet, and made my way back into the house. Sitting my now empty cup on the sideboard, I removed my robe and prepared to sleep soundly.

Farrier

There were so many horses and mules in Carrolltown that I became curious about their care. Understandably, each owner would have to be responsible for their own stock, but inevitably someone would be needed to provide specialized services. Veterinary care was one that came to mind. With all the granite these animals were required to tread upon, there must also be someone who kept them and their hooves healthy on a daily basis. And the more I thought about hooves, the more I wanted to meet the farrier.

In my mind was an image of a muscular blacksmith wearing a leather apron who would forge iron shoes while pumping giant bellows with boot-clad feet. When I walked into the barn where the farrier plied their trade, another of my stereotypes dissolved.

A ginger-haired wiry man with a mouthful of nails held a horse's rear leg between his spindly ones and hammered nails in one by one. The horse seemed nervous, but obviously trusted the man, as he wasn't trying to escape confinement. I watched transfixed as the smithy worked his way around the horse and shod him in an efficient manner.

When he was through, and the horse had been freed to charge about a wood-railed corral, the farrier approached me with a smile on his pale-skinned, freckled face.

"You must be the photographer. I heard you were renting Marlene's place. How do you like our little town so far?"

"A lot," I said sincerely.

"So, what can I do for you? If you need automotive work you'll have to go to Lewisburg. If you want to rent a mule I have two available. Hear tell you're thinking about plowing Marlene's garden under and starting over. Lucy over there (pointing to a nearby stall) is good with people. I'd recommend her."

"Neither at the moment," I said. "I was hoping you'd allow me to watch what you do. I've never been around livestock and am curious about how you manage to shape shoes to such a wide variety of hooves. Do you make them yourself?"

He replied wistfully, as if mourning the passing of a loved one.

"No. I buy them premade from a hardware store in Lewisburg. Our last true blacksmith died thirteen years ago and no one has been able to replace him. I trim their hooves, measure the curves, length and width, then heat the shoes long enough to bend them into the desired shape. I studied mathematics at university, but found that I was a homebody and couldn't plunge into the outside world. I bought the blacksmith shop with a small inheritance and have been working here ever since."

"Are you available every day?" I asked, before realizing it was a redundant question.

"Yes, I am," he said proudly. "Never know when someone might come up lame."

Once again, I was reminded of the symbiosis between man and beast. I looked at Lucy and began to see her as a being who would help, rather than serve me.

I sat in a corner on a hay bale and watched the nimble-fingered man ply his trade. My admiration for him soared over the course of the day. I no longer believed that I could get the photograph I'd been seeking when I came, because physical strength had been surpassed by tenderness. The love, tranquility and consideration Jarrell Thompson applied to his occupation was something born in the heart, and coursed through every vein.

I was tired and ready to leave when a mountainous man in faded coveralls came into the barn, carrying a calf who seemed to have a broken leg. Jarrell rushed forward with his arms outstretched. Taking the calf, he placed it on a workbench that ran along an outside wall.

Before I could ask why the man hadn't taken the calf to the veterinarian, the big man turned to me and said, "Doc Belden is in Lewisburg at a seminar. I can't afford to lose this one. Jarrell here fixed up my missus last year when Nurse Winters was down with the flu."

My photo was of two grim men, both focused on the preservation of a being in pain. No thought beyond that moment. Giving every shred of heart and soul to another.

Community Service

"Leonard Fisher's barn is on fire," a nearly breathless woman said as she rushed into the general mercantile.

I was there because I'd heard that a woman named Marybeth delivered hand-churned butter to the store on Tuesdays, and that by Wednesday it would all be gone. I'd started out thinking butter would be my only purchase, but realized that since the store also served as a postal drop, I could send my aunt in San Francisco some of the delicious jellies, jams and fruit leathers local women proudly displayed on burgeoning shelves.

I'd heard a bell clanging in the distance, but thought it might be a reminder to tardy schoolchildren or church members. That it was a fire bell never entered my mind until the frantic woman began urging the grocer to hurry.

"Sorry, but I have to go," the portly, grey-haired, bespectacled man said. "We all volunteer when there's a fire. The whole town shuts down and everyone helps. You can come back later if you like, but for now, I'll have to ask you to leave."

I had turned and was walking towards the exit when the messenger said, "If you're going to live among us, you should help. That car you have outside could get us there faster than my buggy. Carlton here (pointing to the grocer) is technically our fire chief, even though his bum leg keeps him on the back line these days."

With no second thought, I readily agreed and rushed them to my car. How I could help was a question I had no answer for, but felt sure someone would direct me once on site.

Leonard Fisher lived up a bumpy, winding gravel road. My car's suspension groaned in protest as I kept my foot on the accelerator. When we finally entered a clearing and found the source of smoke that had been tinting the sky ahead of us, I saw a huge wooden barn. One quarter of it was ablaze, and a crowd of people who'd formed a bucket brigade was laboring to save the rest. Looking for the source of the water they were using to douse flames, I saw that nearly forty volunteers had formed a line that reached a nearby creek. A full bucket went forward with one hand. An empty retreated with the other. Bare-chested young men ran perilously towards flames and drenched them, while others raked away coals and covered them with dirt. I stood frozen, not knowing what to do.

"Go help take care of the animals," a man in a one-piece coverall said.

My confusion showed on my face, so he explained.

"All of Leonard's horses and cows are in the corral. They're terrified. We need people to stand among them and keep them calm."

"How do I do that?"

"Just talk to them. Pat a few heads. Rub a flank or two. Hurry! There's still a lot to do."

I propelled myself into the situation without forethought. I simply acted and seemed to be doing well. I walked among animals who might have frightened me before. I found a calm place in myself that I was able to share. The fear in their eyes elicited emotional reactions I'd never felt. It was as if time slowed to a crawl and everything happening around me was in bold relief.

Hours later, Leonard still had half a barn. Tired, dirty people sat in small groups or sprawled alone where they could find purchase. I watched a young girl carry a water bucket around, offering full ladles to those who were thirsty. I watched while three women set up tables, covered them, then placed a wealth of food upon them. Serving dishes and utensils appeared as if by magic. Within minutes, a line of people staggered past and filled their plates. The looks on their faces as they replenished their energies filled me with pride that I had done something to help. Their tradition of staying involved with community and friends moved me to inward silent tears. When I got in line to fill my plate, smiling faces told me that I now belonged. Maybe on probation, but worthy of respect.

The only picture I took that day was of Leonard's barn. Wisps of smoke still escaped it and sunlight streamed through those wisps.

Beads of water were everywhere and the ground was muddy, but the battle had been won. Talk of rebuilding had already surfaced. I shot from the side that was still intact, as I wanted a memento of what can be saved when people stand together against ravages of nature and time.

Sheriff Edwards

The knock on my door was forceful. Something not to be ignored.

Opening it to a strapping, brown-haired, brown-eyed man in a forest-green uniform adorned by multiple badges of authority could have been disconcerting, but I felt no threat or malice from this early morning visitor. Instead, I sensed a person who felt sorry to intrude, but had a job to do.

"Thank you for helping at Leonard's," he said politely, "but I have to give you a warning for a busted taillight. Noticed it yesterday when you were in town."

Reaching out to accept the citation, I said, "Not a problem. I'll go to Lewisburg and have it repaired tomorrow. Very astute of you to notice. It probably got shattered by gravel while I was speeding up the driveway."

"Yeah, most likely," he said. "I really hate to bug you with this, but you're still new here and people talk. If they think I'm slacking, other stuff will happen."

"It's hard for me to imagine much crime here," I stated assertively. "What with the mentality of the people, it would seem to be a safe haven. If you do much more than ticket speeders I would be surprised. When's the last time you had a murder?"

Sheriff Edwards studied me with a jaundiced eye. I felt my value decrease a thousand-fold in an instant. He pondered me more than anyone had in my recent past. I internally counted my multiple flaws. After what seemed an eternity, judgement was rendered. As if granted audience with the Pope, I saw him smile and lean forward with body language meant to initiate me into the inner circle. "1974," he replied. "Guy caught his wife messing around and killed her. Boyfriend too. I was a rookie, but had to interview witnesses and friends. Happy to have nothing much to do these days, though. Like you've figured out, these people prefer doing good deeds."

Feeling we'd reached an understanding, I asked if I could take his picture.

What I wanted was a civil servant who was happy to give his life for greater good. What I got was a man leaning against his cop car, smiling huge teeth at me while I strove for texture, depth and perspective. His cowboy boots were too shiny. His badge too big. His holstered gun more than the job called for. But night after night he patrolled county roads, dedicated to keeping Carrolltown safe. How could I find fault with him for doing his duty, as best as he saw fit?

Commitment

I looked Lucy in the eye and she looked back, wondering what I was planning to feed her. I'd come to know that look and knew she wouldn't leave the enclosure without something to chew.

"Damn you," I said. "Why should I want you in my life? Cleaning up after you. Worrying you might get worms. What about shoes? They don't come cheap, you know? After we turn the soil over, I really should send you back since there's nothing else to do. But, here I am thinking about buying you and being roommates of a sort. What do you think? Am I crazy? I'm a famous photographer, I'll have you know. Burying myself here wasn't part of the original plan. I could fly to Venice tomorrow and be sought after for autographs."

"Where's my corn?" Lucy's dark eyes asked. She'd never heard of Venice and could only pass out hoof prints.

"Damn you," I said. "Don't you understand what I'm going through? These people, AND YOU! You've gotten into my blood. Something important and essential is happening here."

Lucy snorted impatiently. Enough with speeches and on with grub.

Scratching her between the ears, I dug in a bag of mixed corn and oats with the other hand and dumped a hefty portion into Lucy's trough. Adding a chunk of hay, I said, "No work today. Enjoy yourself. I've got shopping to do."

Transition

Fall arrived. Shades of green became tints of ochre, crimson, orange and brown. The school bell summoned and children left behind implements of the fields.

Pumpkins swelled and apples ripened. Nights grew colder and frost covered limbs of trees whose leaves lay scattered before the wind. My fire became more comforting each day as nature began its transition to icy blasts that would come soon.

No longer restless, my daily walks became exploration instead of release. My camera hung around my neck, but rarely did the shutter open and close. My eyes took it all in, and my brain was content simply to observe. I felt comforted, as if held in a loving embrace. Connected to the whispering pulse of life in ways I'd never experienced.

September strode beyond the horizon and Halloween rushed forward. Each house I entered smelled of fresh baked goods, coffee and cocoa. Newly acquired friends stopped by to chat on the porch and share stories of their lives. Axes rang out daily as the need for warmth increased. My car sat forlornly in the driveway, wondering why it had lost its charm. Puffing my way back up the hill with my breath streaming like a cloud of smoke had become exhilarating. How could I explain such feelings to a pile of metal?

Mrs. Hamilton, the school teacher, came by one morning and asked if I would be willing to take pictures of the children this year instead of having cranky old Mr. Barnes drive over from Lewisburg.

Helen Calloway wondered if I might be interested in reviving a monthly newsletter.

People were not just being friendly, but asking me to be involved.

I said no to the newsletter, but was happy to photograph the children. When the appointed day came, I tried my best to capture each of them in as natural a pose as their restless bodies would allow. People offered to pay me for the prints, but I didn't need their money as badly as they. The next time I passed by the school there was a sign in the window saying **"thank you"** that had been signed by all of Mrs. Hamilton's students. How was it that such simple acts of kindness could bring joy to the giver and recipient as well? Had it always been this way, and I hadn't noticed?

Just before Thanksgiving, I looked out my window after stoking the fire and putting my kettle on to boil. Snow had silently crept in overnight and covered everything with white. Nature's paintbrush had once again transformed the constantly changing portrait of Carrolltown. Forgoing my cup of tea, I pulled on my coat and boots, then stood on my hilltop and captured its beauty while it slept.

Gina

"Marlene doesn't want to come back. Fell in love with some Italian guy and wants to ride scooters all over Europe," the slim redhead in a lime-green miniskirt and white go-go boots said.

Introducing herself as Gina, she'd handed me her card, then pushed through my door as if she owned the place. In a way she did. She was a realtor from Lewisburg that Marlene hired to list the house.

"Of course, you get first option since you live here. I wasn't sure if you were planning to stay. Usually by Christmas, renters have gone looking for sun."

It had been gloomy of late, but I didn't mind. I'd discovered a box of books in the attic and found myself staying in socks and pajamas all day, curled up on the couch. Neighbors had taught me to keep a supply of wood drying near the fire, and never forget to cover the pile out back after taking some. A man named Tom had been kind enough to deliver more than I thought I'd need at the time, but his assurances that I would now rang true. Gina looked ridiculous in her skimpy outfit, shivering near the stove, but I guessed her car had a good heater and nice legs could be good for business.

"How soon do you need to know? This is kind of sudden."

"Marlene wants some cash right away, but said she'll carry a note for you. Evidently, when she calls her sister for an update, you get gold stars all around. If I sell it outright and you move, then I make more and she gets a wad she can spend on what's-his-name. Frankly, even though I get less up front, I'd rather sell it to you. Her having all that money scares me."

"Let me think about it for a day," I said, steering her by the elbow towards the door. "I promise to let you know by tomorrow."

"Thanks," she said, taking the hint and grasping the door handle. "To tell the truth, nobody else will buy it right now. Spring maybe.

Who knows? You might not have to move for a long time. Carrolltown is a hard sell to outsiders because of its lack of services. Locals are already settled and seldom relocate. I wouldn't take the listing and drive back and forth if Marlene weren't such a good friend."

Watching Gina mince through a snowbank and jump into her car was the funniest thing I'd seen for a while. It reminded me how much I'd changed and how much more of me remained to be seen. Before she cleared the driveway I'd already made up my mind. Closing out the wind, I picked up my book, then stirred the fire, hoping Lucy missed me and would be for sale instead of being rented by the day.

Portraits of Carrolltown

Part Two
Rescue

My muscles cried out for mercy. Demands on them had become intolerable. My hands had been submerged in icy water so long that my grip was fading and my bones ached. Every part of me except my will wanted to give up. Even if this situation led to my own death, I was unwilling to surrender a young boy to drowning.

I'd attended an ice skating party on New Years' day after spending a peaceful night at home. A bell rang at midnight, but nothing else declared arrival of a new year. Quietude throughout the valley convinced me the passage of time was meaningless when one existed in the here and now. No amount of drinking or celebration would change what work must be done in the morning in order to keep bellies full and stay the creep of chaos. Skating on a frozen river was Carrolltown's equivalent of watching the ball drop in Times Square.

There was a soft spot in the ice. A boy fell through and was clinging to the hardened edge while strong currents tried to sweep him away. I was closest, so I tossed my camera to the side, flopped on my belly and grabbed his underarms. The strain was enormous. I held on valiantly while people procured ropes and advanced to save us both. Ice was cracking and I was losing the battle second by second.

Cold. Bitter cold, as ice beneath me broke away and exposed my belly to the river. We were on the brink of being carried away.

Just as I thought we would go under, a rope reached my hand and I grasped it with all my might. Eventually, the boy and I were pulled to safety by both men and mules heaving on a lifeline, although there were moments when it seemed like their efforts would be in vain. When my feet finally reached solid ground, I trembled with both an adrenaline rush of relief and numbing cold.

Afterwards, people called me a hero, but I did what anyone would do in similar circumstances. It's instinctive. Something in the blood. When I recovered a bit, I took pictures of the hole in the ice where I'd nearly bought the big ticket, and shuddered when I thought about how close I'd come.

My portrait that day was mother and child, holding each other tight in the back of a wagon, tears of joy streaming down their faces. They were waving at a crowd of happy people whose cheeks were also wet with tears. I cried so hard I could barely focus, but somehow my camera delivered at a time when my fingers could barely function. At home, I sat by the fire and relived my experience, wondering if bravery had ever been part of my makeup. Maybe I had learned to be part of something wonderful, and finally understood that self-sacrifice was a quality left dormant in every soul until the moment arrived for it to surface. Placing another log on the flames, I hoped there would never be another occasion when I would be tested in this manner. If so, I would surely hope for something other than an icy plunge into a merciless body of water coursing towards a distant ocean, unmindful of everything swept away in its path

Happenstance

A dead black cat lay in the middle of the road. Were I superstitious, I would have crossed myself, then rubbed my good luck charm and hoped that neither bad tidings nor ill fortune lurked around the next corner. As it was, the poor cat had just chosen the wrong moment to cross the road. This led me to thinking about how happenstance brought me to this isolated corner of the world. What was I doing here? Why had I come? What did I hope to accomplish?

My agent had been calling a lot lately, carping about my lack of production, and separation from a public that (by her definition) was waiting with bated breath for my next presentation. I wasn't the least bit concerned. I had enough work in the bank that I could show in countless galleries for years and not repeat myself. What plagued me was the question of had I peaked? Was my previous work the best I could do?

To satisfy her demands for fresh product, I'd resurrected my car (thanks to a shade-tree mechanic named Bogey, who charged my battery, inflated three flat tires, and tuned up my neglected friend), then set off for Lewisburg with a plan to pillage Radio Shack for every electronic doodad known to man. There was an old sewing room in the house begging for occupancy. Figuring to put it out of its misery, I was planning an office to rival giants of industry. Sadly, what was available in a metropolis as small as Lewisburg landed well below my expectation. Even so, my back seat was filled with bags and boxes as I drove the treacherous twenty-five miles to what I now thought of as home. A dead black cat in the road was not going to hinder me at all.

Housewarming

I thought I was dreaming, but heard it again and crawled out from under the covers. Slipping on a robe, I went to my front window to see what could be causing such clamor. What I saw looked like something from a Christmas card come to life. Three horse-drawn sleighs filled with singing people were coming up my driveway. The horses were in full livery with jingling silver bells attached to every harness and lead. The occupants wore overcoats, or were bundled under heavy blankets, their cheeks red and breath raising clouds of steam as they sang.

The first sleigh was driven by the farrier Jarrell Thompson. The second by Leonard Fisher, whose barn I'd helped save, and the third by Carlton Sykes the storekeeper. I recognized several more of my new friends, waving as they saw my startled face at the window. Unwilling to receive company in my robe, I dropped the curtain and dashed to my room to change.

The stamp of feet on my porch came so quickly that I didn't have time to brush my teeth, but did manage a swig of mouthwash. When I opened the door to my guests, they each held a brightly-wrapped package or bundles that looked suspiciously like food. My stomach growled with anticipation of homemade treats. I had learned what good cooks lived in the valley, and I would welcome such offerings anytime, even if it was a lot like the day the welcome wagon ladies visited. But this felt different.

Dave Martin, the quarryman, was first to speak.

"Heard you bought this place, so we thought a housewarming might be in order. Besides that, you showed us your heart when you saved little Bruce. Mind if we come in?"

By then the porch was crowded, and only Jarrell stood tending the horses. I hoped he wouldn't be left outside in the cold.

"Please do," I said, swinging the door wide and stepping aside.

Presents were piled on a table near the fire, and those mysterious bundles were quickly taken to the kitchen. These people meant business, but were still somewhat out of breath from their songfest. I shook hands with everyone and saw admiration in their smiles.

Within moments, thermos jugs produced steaming hot coffee that had an undertone of brandy. Not real strong, but invigorating. I was wide awake, but still felt like I was dreaming. Somewhat overwhelmed, I was at a loss for words, while others chatted and laughed. Coats came off after I stoked the fire, and people settled on various bits of furniture that came with the house. I was glad I hadn't removed any of it.

At Mrs. Hamilton's urging, I began to unwrap presents with one hand, but then had to finish my coffee and put both hands to the task, or else slop.

"Hope you like it," Carlton Sykes said when I opened a box filled with an assortment of candies from his store. To show my appreciation, I popped a peppermint in my mouth and grinned.

"That's the spirit. Now let's see the rest."

The rest turned out to be a wealth of hand-knitted or woven garments. Colorful scarves, mittens and matching hats. Even two sweaters that were just my size. Leonard Fisher's wife Arlene had shorn the sheep, carded the wool and spun the strands herself. Their work was magnificent, and I almost cried when I thought about these people rocking in their chairs at night, or sitting on a hearth, making gifts for me. I was relieved when Jarrell tramped in and heads turned to welcome him. The distraction allowed me to stealthily wipe my eyes.

"Horses are settled," he said, accepting a cup of the delicious coffee. Taking a flask from his pocket, he added a healthy dollop of brown liquid to it. "Cold out there," he quipped. Everyone laughed.

Most of them had been inside the house while Marlene lived there, but still wandered about, noting changes I'd made. I was worried that my office full of electronics might put them off, but found they understood my need for tools. One thing they all seemed unwilling to do was force their values and lifestyle on anyone. They'd made a choice and found contentment by doing so. I was welcome to stay among them, but would be allowed to remain myself.

"Let's eat!" a woman named Margie, who raised pigs and usually wore galoshes, exclaimed. "I didn't butcher for it to go to waste."

Soon there was a clatter of dishes and silverware. Heaping plates of roast pork, beans, potato salad and at least a dozen other choices were served, and my guests made themselves completely at home while they ate.

"You noticed I didn't bring anything, didn't you?" Dave the quarryman said to me in the kitchen. Running his finger over a linoleum countertop, he continued. "That's because I'd like to give you all new granite to replace these. No charge for labor, or installation either."

I didn't know what to say. He was offering me something of great value and I felt undeserving of such generosity.

"Are you sure?" was all I could manage.

He grinned. "Only if you want it."

Shaking his rock-hard hand reminded me of the night we met. How could I have known such a moment as this would evolve from walking into a diner?

When bellies were full and dishes had been washed and put away, people began to don their coats in preparation for departure. Jarrell had gone out earlier to tend the horses and check rigging. Putting on one of my new sweaters, I followed them and watched as they climbed into their sleighs. My shutter snapped vigorously, trying to capture the scene with my lens. Hands waving, faces smiling, they began to sing as the horses tramped through the snow and their sleighs slid out of sight. In the distance, I could still hear bells as I stood on the porch a moment before returning to my fire.

Peekaboo

Spring stuck its pinky toe and one eye out from under the covers, but wasn't quite ready to leap out of bed and run around naked. Even so, icicles hanging from eaves and bridges began to drip as temperatures slowly rose and winter's frozen grip diminished. Chunks of ice moved downriver and no one risked skating on the remaining thin sheets that were resisting the moment when a new season would arrive in full glory.

Looking in the mirror, I saw that a couple months of lying on the couch and eating delicious leftovers from my housewarming party had created a layer of flab that needed to be walked off. My car was reappearing from yet another blanket of snow, and a few optimistic birds pecked at bared patches of grass for whatever they might find. Baby-blue and rosy-pink began to replace slate-gray skies. Whenever I ventured outside, a few trees dared to produce tiny buds of new growth. Daffodils and tulips, those harbingers of change, thrust tendrils of green through ground that was still half-frozen, but willing to yield to their intrusion. An explosion of rebirth was about to occur. I found myself on tenterhooks, ready to rumble and dying to be involved in whatever lay ahead.

Spring Planting

One of my greatest portraits after the sun came out and mud turned to tillable earth was of Lucy. I'd walked her home from Jarrell Thompson's barn after purchasing her for way less than I knew she was worth. Jarrell offered to bring her, but I wanted to bond with her as we strolled by the river on a beautiful sunny day. She still seemed to like me, and I found I'd missed her a lot.

Now, she was straining at her harness, but turning her head towards me as I held the plow handles like Harlan taught me. She wanted more corn if I wanted to go further. Blackmail of those willing to be deceived. I'd fed her well in the early morn and knew her belly wasn't as empty as proclaimed. Looking directly into her dark pleading eyes, I released one hand and clicked the shutter. I was on to her game.

Later, we sat in the shade of an oak that had erupted in leaves, even though lambs were scarcely birthing. Lucy was working on an ear of dried corn and I held a peanut butter sandwich. My evil thought was that Lucy was stuck with water at the end of day, where I was going to have a frosty-cold beer.

I was doubtful as I poked seeds into the ground. Instructions on the packages said conditions were right for my zone, but nights were still cold and frost appeared periodically. I persevered though, while Lucy watched me like I was a blooming idiot. Little did she know that I was including her next winter's feed in my planting.

A song rose in my heart. It entered my mind and I was stilled. Serenity crept into my soul and I felt fulfilled. I thought fleetingly of harvest, but focused instead on the joyous surge from below. Voyaging into light, but grounded in mother earth. Reaching into the void for sustenance, in order to surrender ensuing bounty.

Self-definition

I feel that I am but a lens. Peering into light and shadow, trying to grasp a true picture of what stands in front of me. I am an observer, often guilty of not being involved.

That is changing though. I now truly care about those around me. I felt bad when Homer Winslow's horse died and his buggy sat idle. Put money in the hat when Harriet Parks had to bury her husband. I'd trod a mile in my fellow man's shoes and found myself understanding the concept of being both footsore and desolate, yet determined to winnow what meager gains could be wrought from life. What I could do to help Carrolltown move forward remained to be seen.

My chance to be useful came at a time when my garden was reaching for the sky and every meadow I walked past was filled with flowers and new grass. Foals stood by their mothers, or romped while kicking spindly legs in the air.

Trinidad Carroll, an unmarried descendant of old Flavius Carroll, the town founder, came to ask if I wanted to be on a committee planning the annual spring picnic. I'd just sent my agent some new work and was momentarily at a loose end, so I said yes.

Trinidad lived in what could be called a mansion. Evidently, she and her relatives still had some of the family money, so she was rumored to be filthy rich. Tongue-wagging gossips were known to say that the reason she never married was an unwillingness to share the spoils with a suitor who might be seeking a soft spot to land. Others said she was butt-ugly and hadn't had a date in decades. Whatever the reason, I found her to be pleasant company while we planned menus and created a list of assignments. A growing roster of names made me realize how few of the residents I'd actually met.

One of the people working on the committee was fascinating. Within moments of meeting her, I knew she would be my next portrait. Time and place were not conducive to what I had in mind, however, and it took a while to get invited to her home. That was what I needed, and looked forward to time alone with her.

Collen Carroll-Dawes

She'd been famous in her time. A movie star without a sordid lifestyle, or a string of ex-lovers who spoke badly of her in tabloids. She'd been, and still was, noble, gracious and kind, as well as beautiful. One of the only Carrolls who'd traveled far from home, she'd returned to Carrolltown after the death of her husband. Taking up residence in an entirely wooden home along Main Street (the majority were mostly granite), she now volunteered for events such as I'd helped plan, as well as driving to Lewisburg once a month to teach an acting class (weather providing). Stepping into her home, I smelled lavender, a touch of cinnamon, and strong Ethiopian coffee she'd brewed for the occasion. Shaking my hand with a feather-light touch, she ushered me to an upholstered wingback chair, while placing her slender but strong vital body on a scalloped maroon velvet couch with carved wooden edgings and legs. The entire room was filled with exotic fabrics softly glistening in muted light. Some hanging, like Salome's veils, others covering mullioned windows to provide privacy. The wallpaper was gilded and tufted. Elegance reached out to my eyes and kissed them softly.

After pleasantries were exchanged, and coffee served, she bored into me with amber orbs that made men swoon and audiences weep. "Why do you want to take my picture? There are thousands of them around the world. Maybe millions. I lost count."

"Not a picture exactly. A portrait of who you are now. As to why? I find you fascinating. Not everyone from such a small town has what it takes to be a film star."

She blushed slightly. "I suppose you're right. They came from everywhere, those poor girls. Terrible things happened to so many of them. Some simply found a good husband or went home. I was lucky."

"You had talent to go with your beauty."

She sighed wistfully. "Had I not met Parker Dawes, I might have fallen by the wayside as well. How much do you know about me?"

"Truthfully, I only became aware of you while working on Trinidad's committee. She told me a few things, but most of what I know came from the Internet. I did watch two of your films on Netflix. You went to City College in Lewisburg, starred in a few plays, and met the man you would marry while he was visiting relatives and attended one of those plays."

She seemed pleased. Amber eyes sparkled. "Very good. But I didn't run off with him like some people are fond of saying. After he invited me to audition for an upcoming part, my aunt took me to Los Angeles by train and supervised every meeting until a contract was signed. He was considered the top agent for young talent and could have married anyone he chose. That he fell in love with me and guided my career was a blessing worth more than all the gold we gathered."

Sipping her coffee, she studied me for a moment. "I suppose you want me to pose. I hate that, you know? All those lights, sweaty foreheads and stage props. Now that I'm ninety, every wrinkle shows."

Her skin was like fine porcelain. Her silver hair shimmered with health. Her scant makeup was completely understated. Her teeth were her own and straight as could be. Women would kill for such graceful aging.

"No props. No staging. I'd just like to come over from time to time and observe your day-to-day activities. When the moment is right, I'll take advantage. I know I'm asking a lot and could become a pest. If you say no, I'll understand."

Stretching like a cat, she rose, then walked to a Chippendale sideboard that collectors would pay a fortune for. Sliding open a slender drawer, she removed a key. Turning towards me, she paused, thought, gripped it, and then surrendered it to my outstretched hand. "This opens the side gate. My day-to-day activities are among my flowers. Come quietly. I'll speak if I like, but do not intrude if I seem lost in memory. Do we have a deal?"

"Absolutely."

I was ecstatic, and felt like jumping with joy. Not wanting to overstay my welcome, I said, "I'll let myself out. You've been very kind."

I had my hand on an antique brass doorknob when she said, "Make sure I get a signed first edition. I've researched you as well."

Doc Belden

I was frantic as I sprinted for the house to call Doc Belden. After days of howling wind and torrential rains that not only cancelled the spring picnic and quelled virtually all outdoor activities, I'd gone to her enclosure and found Lucy lying on the ground, bloated like she'd swallowed a beach ball. She was gasping for breath, obviously in pain, and looked at me with fear-filled eyes. I was at a loss as to what to do for her.

During the storm, we'd both stayed inside, as we couldn't work while the river overflowed its banks, landslides blocked roads and power went off for hours at a time. Thankful that phone lines were not down, I listened with growing impatience as the other end rang and rang with no answer. Finally, when I was nearly at my wits' end, a woman answered.

"Carrolltown Clinic. This is Nurse Winters. How can I help?"

My words tumbled out in a furious rush as I explained the problem, hoping Doc Belden was available, lest Lucy die.

"Road's blocked. Power lines are sparking everywhere. Tough to get around. Doc is outside, bandaging a dog that got swept downstream and hit the bridge. So far today, we've had a rollover crash with two broken legs, a baby delivery and a cow that got tangled in barbwire. Could be hours before he can get there. You ever treated colic?"

"No. Lucy is the first animal I've ever owned. Please! If there's anything you can do."

Tears filled my eyes as silence filled the line.

"I'll let him know. Don't get your hopes up. Meanwhile, see if you can get her on her feet. Walking helps."

When the line went dead, I felt a sense of helplessness I'd never experienced. Filled with anxiety and dread, I made my way back to Lucy and urged her to stand. When she wouldn't, I prepared for the worst. Was I to lose my friend? Stroking her between the ears, I waited for the doctor to come.

It seemed like an eternity before I heard hooves clattering on my driveway. Rushing back to the house, I was overjoyed to see a tall, sandy-haired man climbing down from a pinto horse. It had started to rain again and he wore a clear plastic poncho over a blood-stained tunic. His boots were covered with mud and the horse quivered with exhaustion.

"Where is she?" he asked.

"Out back," I replied.

There was no time for formalities.

Tethering his horse to my porch rail, he patted its sides, whispered into its ear, fed it a treat, and then followed me to Lucy's enclosure.

"Overeating," he said.

I remembered then that she'd raided the corn supply during the storm, when I'd been distracted.

"Lack of exercise and a bit dehydrated. Looks like some of your hay is moldy."

Turning his intense green eyes on me caused me to shrink with embarrassment.

"Not your fault. Jarrell should have taught you better. Problem is, she's got a bad blockage. I'm gonna have to reach in and break it down. I'll need you to hold her while I work. Nurse Winters would normally have come along, but we're swimming in problems today."

Two hours later, after using a nasogastric tube and donning elbow-length neoprene gloves to massage her intestines, Lucy stood up and passed gas for at least twenty minutes. A flood of excrement followed.

"She'll be okay now, but you need to get rid of all this feed. Besides being contaminated, it's too much temptation. I'd recommend you keep it out of her sight and reach. Feed her less and walk her more. Don't spoil her so much. It's not cruelty to keep her from overindulging. When she's working hard, give her more, but keep the feed off the ground and well ventilated so it doesn't grow mold."

"You look exhausted," I said, as we walked towards the house. "How about hot coffee and something to eat?"

He looked at me candidly. I could tell he felt obligated to move on to other things, but we'd never had a chance to get acquainted. He was curious, tired and hungry, so he accepted my invitation.

"Are you both veterinarian and doctor?" I asked, once we were comfortably settled and had food on our plates.

His mouth was full, so he nodded.

"Why?" I asked. Working in one field would be challenging. Understanding disparate physiologies and ailments would be genius.

Setting his plate aside, and wiping his mouth, Doc Belden leaned back in his chair. He took a sip of coffee, then drilled me with those green eyes.

"We had a doctor until a few years ago. I trained as a vet, but was always curious about people. When Carl Flagstaff died, I was all there was. Folks started coming to me with cuts and bruises, then it was babies and breast cancer. Anything I couldn't handle, I farmed out to the hospital in Lewisburg, but that's a long drive to most. You have to understand that these people don't want outside intervention. They're not Luddites or religious fanatics, but simply infatuated with their own way of life. Having me take care of them, and their animals as well, is comforting. Situations like the last few days make me look forward to the day Harlan and Sarah's son Caleb graduates and hangs his shingle here in Carrolltown."

I felt we were just getting to know each other when my phone rang. Nurse Winters needed the doctor to help with three victims of a landslide. Carrying my camera with me, I followed him outside and watched while he pulled a carrot from a leather saddlebag and fed it to his stalwart companion. As he swung his leg over the saddle, I captured him. A man on a mission, dedicated to saving lives.

Word Storms

Sacrificing his own comfort to provide it to others.

War Hero

Walter Clemens sat on a wooden bench outside the general mercantile every day of the week when the weather was nice. Shriveled with age, he wore high-waist khaki pants and a blue chambray shirt, festooned with service ribbons across a sunken chest. He'd served proudly, and would display his scars to anyone who asked to see them. He was the only veteran of foreign wars from the area, so there was no fraternity to join. He was alone with his memories.

    I saw him frequently as I became more involved with Carrolltown. We spoke about armament and the roar of cannons when I had time, but mostly, he just sat in the sun, submerged in the past. I felt badly that he had no wife or family to provide diversion. I usually brought him donuts and he would eat them slowly while regaling me with stories from his days of service. He was a memento of a time when people believed they were the force of goodness and the devil supported the other side. Even though I believed otherwise, he was a poignant reminder of their desire for a better future.

    Serendipitously, I took his picture the day before he died. Sheriff Edwards found him the next morning, clasping a ribbon he'd been awarded for bravery. How different they were, these men. Leaving home and loved ones, boarding a train, then marching off to war. Singing songs of inspiration, even though their ultimate fate was to be lonely old men like Walter, wearing their medals and sitting on benches everywhere.

Moonshine Man

Ezekiel Mallard was a local legend. Evidently, he'd migrated from Appalachia to Carrolltown with A.T.F. agents hot on his heels. He'd taken up farming long enough to avoid prosecution, but once freed from scrutiny went back to making some of the best moonshine on planet earth. He was reputed to be combative, reclusive and territorial. According to wagging tongues at Todd's Place, the only way to buy his product was to stand at the end of his driveway and pass inspection. If he didn't like your whiff, you left emptyhanded. The tavern served none of his product, so I had yet to taste his wares, but became more curious about him as time passed.

Deciding to take the bull by the horns, I set out walking one afternoon, and took on the precipitous dirt road leading to his property. A dazzling row of maples lined the way as I climbed from river level to dizzying heights. Brambles grew thick, and light dimmed at times, due to dense tree cover, even though skies were clear and brilliant blue. I huffed and puffed my way to the top of a spiny granite ridge, and found myself standing before a narrow track that could be called a driveway if one commuted by horse or bicycle. No car could traverse its rutted, serpentine course to a shack that leaned as if it were in danger of collapsing any moment. A locked steel gate and a barbwire fence nailed to thick wooden posts barred anyone from attempting its challenge.

As if he were psychic, and knew I would come, Ezekiel Mallard stood behind that gate with a .12 gauge shotgun held at port arms. He looked the part. Bib overalls, long gray beard, heavy brogues, and hate-filled eyes.

Amazingly, he knew who I was. "You're that photographer. Whaddya want? There's nothing here for you. The best thing you could do would be to turn around and go back where you came from."

"What if I wanted to buy some shine?"

His laugh was a dry cackle. "Think I believe that? You just want to invade everyone's privacy, then go sell your pictures and make a bunch'a money. You don't fool me. Now get on outta here, 'fore I lose my temper."

Should I plead my case? Tell him how much I'd come to love the town? Should I tell him to keep his liquor and shove it in a dark place? How did I really feel about someone challenging my right to live among them and capture their essences?

Walking home, seemingly emptyhanded, I noticed lichens invading granite outcrops. Trees regenerating after searing fire. I noticed ferns growing by the wayside. Saw a ruminant plowing through underbrush, hoping I would not be in pursuit with a weapon. Nature soothed my wounded pride, and I felt more committed than ever to being a good neighbor. My business was my business, but my personal focus had shifted. I became interested. I began to care. Fate led me to this moment, and I sought to understand its meaning.

Ezekiel Mallard didn't know that I owned a telephoto lens. An outcropping about halfway down allowed me a clear view of him, cutting the corner off a plug of tobacco, and raising it to his lips.

A Favor

"It's wonderful!" Colleen Carroll-Dawes said, as she gazed at her portrait. I'd captured her kneeling by her small backyard fishpond, holding a bouquet of fresh-cut flowers cradled in one arm, while feeding the fish with her other hand. Sunlight streamed through low-lying clouds right after a rain shower. She was wearing a long garden apron and had the sleeves of a flannel shirt rolled up to her elbows. One button was missing and only half of the collar was turned down. A well-worn straw hat perched jauntily on her head. Her beautiful face was filled with serene happiness, reminiscent of a renaissance painting. She hadn't noticed me that day and I seized my chance to catch her unawares.

I'd invited her to tea at my home, both to give her the poster-sized print and show off my office workshop. She was impressed by my growing collection of Carrolltown portraits and said so, but I sensed something else was on her mind.

"I need you to do me a favor," she said, reaching for a second butter cookie.

There it was. Out in the open.

Taking my silence as a cue to continue, she did. "I've always wanted a great picture of my sister Trinidad to hang in our ancestor gallery. It's upstairs, and I should have shown it to you, but I seldom allow anyone beyond the room where I greeted you that first day. Now I feel remiss, since you have shown yourself to be of sterling character. Next time you visit I'll show it to you."

"I'd love to see it, but you know I don't take posed portraits. I would assume many of your ancestors sat in their finery while a photographer fussed over details."

"Yes. Many of them are stern, with eyes as unyielding as the granite they quarried. But not all. Some of the women will surprise you with their coquettishness. I'm not asking you to compromise your ethics. Trinidad is more of a public figure than I, and I would like you to take one of the many opportunities her lifestyle will provide and freeze it in time."

I sipped my tea while I thought. If I did this, would there be an endless line of such requests? As if reading my mind, she said. "It will remain between us. No one needs to know. Her portrait will hang where only the two of us can view it. As you know, we are both ancient and will pass eventually. The next in line may sell the house and consider family portraits irrelevant. I have no control over that. For the moment, I'd like to see Trinidad among her predecessors. Could you do this for me?"

How can one say no to a sweet old lady with her hand wrapped daintily around a teacup and an imploring look in eyes that captivated millions? My gut churned, and I felt faint stirrings of a headache. Was this the life junction that ultimately led me astray, or was I being melodramatic about doing a favor for a friend?

"Okay," I said, after a lengthy pause. "But only if a situation arises where I can give it my personal stamp. Friendship or no, my art is me."

"I would never ask anyone for their soul. I never gave mine to anyone but my husband, and he considered it a loan. Should the occasion never arise, I will understand, but will you promise to look for it?"

At that moment, we understood each other clearly. All I could do was smile and offer her more tea.

Fourth of July

Rain cancellation of the spring picnic created a feverish desire in Carrolltown to party. They'd planned menus, delegated chores, but all for naught. Now, the sun was high, and all signs pointed to a joyous good time. Casseroles were baked, pies as well, and a score of potato salads lay waiting in refrigerators across town. Smiles abounded. Chores were set aside. Horses and mules grazed on knee-high grass. Red, white and blue bunting adorned a stage where the school band would play. Fireworks crackled above the sounds of buggies gathering at town square.

Upon arrival, I wandered freely amid the revelry, and after two hours I'd sampled so much food, my belly swelled and complained. Sitting on a bench to recover, I smiled at hundreds of new acquaintances and friends as they passed. I had never felt so accepted in my life. Scores of admiring fans at gallery shows could bloat one's ego, but gaining respect from such reclusive people was treasure of separate worth.

I was nearly catatonic when Trinidad walked by. She was wearing a colorful peasant dress and sturdy leather sandals. Her hair was braided, then wrapped around her head and pinned. Her eyes glowed as if she were in a euphoric state. Drugs? I doubted so. She was just letting it all hang out. Everyone was having fun and squeals of happy children filled the air. It seemed that each attendee wore a grin like hers.

Remembering I still had an errand, I got up from the bench and started following her around. I said I'd do a favor and was now bound to do so.

As described by her sister, she was a social butterfly, flitting from group to group in almost non-stop conversation. I found myself getting frustrated at the lack of proper angle and setting. Trying desperately to keep my cool, I reminisced about waiting in jungle for hours, hoping for a rare tiger to make an appearance at a watering hole. It wasn't working very well, and I was ready to give up and go home.

Just then, she broke away from a group, went behind a tent, and sat on a three-legged stool. Her face showed fatigue as she wrapped the hem of her dress tightly around her ankles, then leaned against the tent wall. I watched quietly while she rested her eyes for a few minutes. When they blinked open, she sat upright and began unbraiding her hair. Pulling a brush from her handbag, she began applying it to her tresses in long, even strokes. Her face lost its haggard look and she started to hum in low tones. Moments later, she radiated that same serenity I'd admired in her sister. Beatific would be a one-word description.

I caught the sparkle in her eyes, and sunlight dancing off her hair, while a playful breeze blew a few strands across her cheek. Afterwards, I watched the tug-of-war and horseshoe pitching, then bought a cake from old Mrs. Mabley, who was considered the best baker in town. Carrying the box gently on my way home, I thought about what Ezekiel Mallard said to me at the top of his driveway. Was I really just an exploiter who had deluded their self, and that time spent here was only about money and further acclaim? Did I care enough about these people's welfare to not share their portraits with the outside world? An ugly vision of Winnebagos parked all over town seared my brain. Tourists asking the quaint people to pose so little Sally could share on Facebook. Would, or could I, be responsible for the death of simplicity and tranquility?

San Francisco

"You need to fly here so we can talk about your future. If you want me to keep representing you, I want face to face over a good lunch."

So began the phone conversation with Diane, my agent. I knew she was bluffing about leaving, but also knew she was deserving of attention. Since arriving in Carrolltown I hadn't strayed far, although I'd sent Diane plenty of work. At the moment, I was about to open in Sao Paulo, and in Amsterdam next month. My bank account was fine, pantry full, and I was having a wonderful summer. Flying off wouldn't be fun, but I understood. Sighing, I said, "Okay. I'll be there Wednesday. Pick me up?"

"Text me the flight number," was all she said before hanging up.

So, here I was, sitting in a steakhouse, looking out at the Bay Bridge and a sky full of puffy clouds and seagulls. Diane looked resplendent as always, with auburn hair cut in an A-frame. Hazel eyes punched holes in me, while glossy nails tapped the tabletop with impatience.

Frustration filled her voice. "What do you mean, you won't release the Carrolltown photos? Not finished? Not good enough? Talk to me."

"I mean they are not for public display at all. After I'm dead I can't stop you from hanging them, but meanwhile, I don't want to share Carrolltown. It's too beautiful to defile with exposure."

"That's crap. What happened? Fall in love? Hit your head on a rock? I'm not buying this."

"Sorry. The swell of interest would ruin those people's way of life. I'm accepted as one of them and love my new home. I plan to keep my apartment here for when you really need my presence, but from now on, I'm asking you to forget Carrolltown and not disclose my whereabouts."

"Wow! That's brutal. We've worked together a long time. Why ruin a good thing?"

"I'm not breaking off with you or giving up my career. I'll come out for good shoots. Just tell me where and when to be, with ample notice. No quickie appearances to fundraise or that kind of stuff. Believe it or not, I have a bag for you in my room, filled with vegetables I grew. You might not understand my desire for secrecy, but I'm counting on your personal integrity to respect my wishes. You won't suffer any loss of revenue."

"That's not the point."

"Then what is?"

Peevishly, she replied, "The point is that you're taking yourself out of circulation. The gallery owner in Sao Paulo was disappointed at not meeting you and showing you off. Right now, people want your work. Will it stay that way if you become a hermit? Part of the gig is that the public feels they have a right to some type of personal interaction with you. Signing autographs and shaking hands is the key to more sales."

I had to laugh. "I'm far from being a hermit, but I get your drift."

Angered further by my outburst, she continued. "Have you ever considered that I am not just in it for the money and might view you as a friend whose interests I look out for?"

"Sure I have. But this is not about you and me. It's simply about me. I'm happy. I eat well and sleep soundly. No traffic noise. No airplane roar. Air so clear you can see the stars. I can't sully that in good conscience."

"Lunch is getting cold," Diane said, viciously attacking her steak.

Home

Looking at my row of corn, I could swear it had grown six inches while I was gone. Lucy seemed genuinely happy to see me and nuzzled my cheek. Tomatoes hung heavy and ripe, and my pumpkins were larger. I noticed a crack in the driveway that would need attention soon. A section of fence was getting a bit saggy. One shutter seemed to hang crookedly. There were definitely things to do. Looking down at Carrolltown, my heart rate slowed and calmness washed over me. So many happy times with good people reaffirmed my decision not to betray the trust bestowed on me. I knew it could not remain this way forever, but for the moment, hills were green and beauty filled every horizon. I was at peace, but as always, Lucy was begging for something to chew.

* * * *

Workers Unite
By Howard Schneider

World Tribune International: Tuesday, March 8, 2024

Madrid: Yesterday, at the annual Prehistoric Legal History Society meeting, scientists reported archeological evidence of trade goods and related business transactions in prehistoric Spain. Collectively, the findings represent a major contribution to an origin of legal practice in ancient times. These discoveries, uncovered from deep recesses of the Altamira Caves in central Spain, date to 45,000 BC.

The head researcher, Dr. Lizara Habanero (Chairwoman, Department of Prehistoric History, University of Madrid), speculated that such trade activities would have had to employ barter and negotiation. It can, she claims, be assumed that these "cavemen" would have required the services of lawyers. Reported by her colleague on the excavation team, Dr. Hillarius Schmidt (Professor of Anthropology, University of Cologne), chiseled stone tablets discovered in a nearby cave in Southern Spain support Habanero's assumption; they appear to be records of chargeable hours and case notes for a client involved in wholesaling flint spear points and related flintknapped items to a distributor headquartered in the area now known as Barcelona.

Computer scientists on the team, using Microsoft's prehistoric language translation software and Google's prehistoric map algorithms, determined from these records that a law firm named Muuk, Gork and Uck was retained by a business entity called Mooga Flint Works to negotiate transfer pricing and limits of liability for a contract between Mooga and a giant retail chain named Cavemart. The records further revealed that the transaction took a nasty turn when Mooga's lead lawyer, identified as Gorg Goldberg, discovered that Cavemart attempted to bribe Mooga's Vice President for marketing to obtain favorable prices. Cavemart denied the charges and counter-sued with a claim of false accusation.

Faced with a prolonged trial, the parties agreed to an out-of-court settlement. Habanero speculated that Mooga probably lacked the financial resources to pursue an expensive legal battle, and, based on additional archeological evidence, that Cavemart may have already been encountering public resentment over its policy of low pay and no overtime for its Neanderthal warehouses workers. Cavemart may have also feared that information would be made public about its success in preventing its workers from forming a union: the tablets indicated that Cavemart had previously fired the 50% of its workers who supported unionizing.

According to Habanero, at that time the procedure for resolving out-of-court legal settlements was to pit five of the eldest members of each litigant against each other in armed battle. The winner was the team that had the most combatants remaining upright by the time the sand drained out of a large gourd (two hours and seven minutes, as determined by laboratory studies). Each team could select weapons from whatever items their employer sold, manufactured or happened to have lying around. Admission to the public spectacle was free, and attendance was always heavy when legal settlements such as this were conducted.

It would seem that Mooga Flint Works, being in the spear point business, would have an advantage over the Cavemart employees; they would have been familiar with the use of weapons and would likely have welcomed an opportunity to prove their skill and bravery. As recorded in the case notes, when Mooga's management staff, which was younger than its factory workers, and therefore not qualified to participate in the battle, requested volunteers, the shop steward referred them to the president of their union, The United Flint Workers. It is interesting that the records also described a large wage increase at Mooga just after the Cavemart litigation was settled. Irrespective of the reason, five Mooga factory workers volunteered, all over the age of fifty-five, still vigorous, and highly accomplished in martial arts. Three were Neanderthals, and the other two were regular Homo sapiens.

Cavemart, on the other hand, as the deposition record shows, relied on cunning rather than martial proficiency to settle the dispute. Their Human Resources Department used a psychodynamic profiling questionnaire to choose their combatants based on deviousness, lack of moral values, dishonesty and greed, all characteristics that reflected Cavemart's management-level hiring requirements.

The records provide a detailed description of the event. The arena opened at 10 a.m. and was filled by 11. The battle began at mid-day and would last until the sand ran out, unless, that is, all five on each side were still standing. In that case, the battle would continue until the first man went down, and stayed down.

The combatants entered the field at 11:55 and lined up opposite each other. They were stripped to the waist, clad only in leather breeches and sturdy sandals. Wild patterns and animal likenesses were painted on their faces and torsos. Each man held a weapon in one hand and a shield in the other. An assortment of additional weapons hung from wide belts around their waists. Animal-pelt caps adorned their heads.

Precisely at high noon, as signified by the public sundial, a gong was struck, the timer gourd inverted, and the battle commenced.

Determined to bring about a swift conclusion to the contest, the Mooga men took the initiative and quickly dropped their shields and notched their spears into their atlatls and, in what seemed like split seconds, sent a barrage of fury hurling towards the Cavemart ranks. But, to the surprise of the Mooga men, the Cavemart men reacted just as quickly. Having anticipated such an obvious attack, they raised their shields and deflected the oncoming spears that kicked up dust as they landed ineffectively in the dirt.

The Cavemart forces immediately picked up the Mooga spears, positioned them low in front of them and rushed headlong towards the surprised Mooga opponents. The Mooga men grabbed hold of mammoth-bone clubs hanging from their belts and met the charging opponents by knocking the spears away, then stepped aside as the momentum of the charging attackers carried them past the Mooga line, spears flailing uselessly in the air or plunging to the ground. The Mooga fighters twisted around and charged after the Cavemart men, effortlessly clubbing them to submission. It was no contest. The Cavemart men, apparently wounded beyond recovery and scattered on the ground, acknowledged defeat and pleaded for mercy. The Mooga fighters, assuming victory, and being of a magnanimous nature, dropped their clubs and prepared to help take the defeated Cavemart adversaries to the infirmary.

Not suspecting subterfuge by the Cavemart men, the trusting Mooga men were caught off guard when the first of them, a well-meaning Neanderthal named Fook, knelt to make sure that the wounded Cavemart soldier was still alive. In a flash, the Cavemart man, who was only pretending to be unconscious, slipped a razor-sharp obsidian knife from his scabbard and plunged it into Fook's midsection, driving it under his ribs and into his heart. Fook died instantly. During the quick thrust, the Cavemart man's leather cap fell off to reveal a bone head-covering he wore underneath, the same as his companions did. The helmets, carved from cave bear skulls, had protected them from the Mooga clubs. In the confusion, another of the Cavemart combatants did the same thing, killing a second Mooga man. The other Mooga fighters jumped back and out of reach, retrieved their clubs and regrouped. It was then three of them against five Cavemart men, each of whom held a long, black, deadly-sharp obsidian knife in his hand.

Realizing the risk of close combat, especially against greater odds, the Mooga men cautiously moved back to where their spears lay, picked them up and stood facing the slowly advancing Cavemart combatants, their knives held out in front of them, slicing the air back and forth. Then, on a silent signal from the leader, the three Mooga men hurled their spears, two of which found their targets with lethal accuracy, while the third was deflected by the Cavemart man's knife. It was then three against three, knives against clubs, the ranks separated by a five-yard gap.

The crowd was nearly delirious with excitement and urged the fighters on to further combat. Empowered by the exuberance of the onlookers, the Mooga men rushed forward in a wild rage. They deftly knocked the long knives aside and repeatedly and mercilessly pummeled the floundering Cavemart managers with their clubs. Superior martial skill and unyielding resolve resulted in the Mooga union men thoroughly decimating the Cavemart executives, and, in so doing, uncontestably settled the legal case in their favor. Not only did this victory result in a hefty payment to Mooga, but thwarted the nascent threat of Cavemart management's attempts to abolish the rights of their workers.

When asked about the significance of this discovery, the noted Harvard philosopher, Geraldine Gerts, issued the following statement:

The precedent this historic battle established for workers' unions endured four hundred centuries. But, seats of power shifted, wealth concentrated in fewer hands, and its influence was magnified and perverted. And so, some forty thousand years later, that hard-won union power was finally overcome by unfettered greed. But, as we have sadly come to realize, such is the way of modern man. A constant tug-of-war between good and evil, between corruption and fairness. The question now is what lies ahead. The answer to which, no one knows. But is for all of us to decide.

Hello Seniors
By Howard Schneider

"Helloo seniors . . . I have help for you," a soothing and melodious male voice said when Lilly picked up the receiver.

"Don't hang up!" I yelled from the living room as I sprang from my chair and tossed the paper aside.

"It's that same man," Lilly said, as I ran into the kitchen where she held the phone in her outstretched hand.

"Yeah. Thought it might be. He always calls about this time. I'll take it. I'm gonna end these calls once and for all!"

"You really gonna answer it?" she said.

"You bet I am. I want to find out who he is and make him take our number off his stinking call list. I've had it with this bullshit."

"Good luck with that," she said, as I grabbed the phone.

"Don't worry. I can handle it," I replied, then said into the mouthpiece, "Who is this?" trying to sound authoritarian.

There was no reply, just the silence of electrons jumping from one gap to the next, making connections, finding an opening.

Then, after a few seconds, just before my patience gave out and I hung up, a human came on the line. A female. From the crinkle in the link, she felt far away, on the other side of the world.

"Is this Mr. Frederick?" I recognized the accent immediately; she was in a far-away country. But her enticing voice rang with a musical quality so inviting that I was momentarily stunned, unable to unleash the verbal assault I had planned. I recovered quickly, though, refusing to be lulled into submission by the allure of vocal perfection, not forgetting I had a job to do. To make whoever it was leave us alone. To stop these unrelenting telephone attacks. "Who are you?" I countered.

"I am Jane, and I have an important message for Mr. Frederick. Are you Mr. Frederick Shi . . . Shnee . . . Sheyder?"

"It's Schneider! Yes! That's me. Why are you calling and what organization it this?"

"Mr. Frederick. You sound so angry. Please don't be that way. Let me be your friend. I am only wanting to talk with you because we want to help you."

"Who's we?" I said, not responding to her snake-like friendliness.

"Mr. Frederick. First, let me say how happy I am to be able to talk with you. How are you today? I see from my weather chart that it is now raining in your fine city of Portland O R. Are you enjoying the cool temperature?"

"Look. I know where you're calling from and that you want to sell me something. And I don't care to discuss the weather. The only thing I want is my name and number taken off your call list. I don't want any more calls from your company. Will you do that, please?"

"I am sorry, Mr. Frederick, sir. I am not allowed to take your information away. That is not my job. I can explain how we can help you only. May I please do that?"

"No! I don't want your help. I don't need it. Unless you can delete my number. That's all I want. All I need. Do you understand?"

"Good sir. I am becoming worried about you. Have you tried meditation to control your anger? Or perhaps yoga? It too can be effective. Even my good father found them of great help before he died from high pressure of the blood."

"Jane! Or whatever your damn name is. My anger's none of your business. And I'm not angry! And I don't care about your father. I'm just frustrated by your damn calls, three times a day, every day. I want them to stop! And stop now!"

"Mr. Frederick. If you remain angry like this and shout at me I will have to report your verbal abuse to the authorities. I am calling to help you only. You are instead treating me so very badly."

"I'm not treating you badly!" I screamed. Then, recovering a little calm, and with groveling self-control, I said, "I am simply requesting that my name and number be removed from your call list. That is all I want."

"I understand, Mr. Frederick. But, as I already told you, I am not allowed to do that. Would you like to speak with my supervisor? He could explain the process for submitting requests of that nature. But if I transfer you to him without you letting me explain how we can help you, I will get into a great amount of trouble. Do you really want to let your anger destroy my career?"

"Jane, I don't want to speak to anyone else. I don't want to hear about how you can help me. I just want off your goddamn fucking list!"

Click! The line was cut. Dead. Jane was gone, with nothing but silence in her place.

I slammed the phone down and returned to my chair, my heart rate higher than it should be, and yes, smoldering with anger at my failure to achieve what I had set out to.

Twenty minutes later, the phone rang. I let Lilly get it.

"It's for you," she yelled from the back room.

"Who is it?" I yelled back.

"A Mr. Keen. Said he's with the FBI. The International Telephone Terrorism Division. He doesn't sound very happy."

Archie

By Mizeta Moon

I never wanted to be homeless, but years of grueling work left me injured and unemployable. I'd been a private contractor paying nothing into the system, so the state of California wasn't interested in helping me. They had plenty of others in line already. San Diego was a horrible place to find oneself on the streets, so I drifted to San Francisco, where a highly democratic attitude produced a wealth of services for the homeless. Much the same as in Portland today, the sidewalks became littered with unwashed, and often drunken or drug-stupefied bodies. There were free meals available at most hours of the day, and kind-hearted people volunteered medical, clothing and grooming services to everyone they could afford to help.

It didn't take me long to disassociate myself from professional beggars, thieves and those who lived on the streets by choice and felt it was their right to be taken care of by others. Almost all of them smoked endless cigarettes while complaining about the quality or content of free meals and waiting in long lines. Once the word got out about how much free stuff was available, more of them came from less friendly parts of the country. I gratefully ate what was given, said please and thank you, then went somewhere that I could be alone and read books I scavenged from recycling bins, or write poetry. I had no friends on the streets and didn't want any.

I've never believed in panhandling, so I did what lots of others did for money, which was to collect bottles and cans. Regular people often looked into my eyes and told me I didn't belong out there. They saw that I was intelligent and wasn't angling for a lifelong free ride. Explaining that I needed time to heal before rejoining the workforce, they sensed my truthfulness and would put a twenty in my hand so that I could shower and wash my clothes. I prided myself on not being unkempt and used my recycling money to keep my bedroll fresh and buy myself a beer or two at the end of day.

My recycling led me to Archie. He was a homeless black man who pushed a cart around like I did. I ran into him quite a bit, since we sold at the same location. He had two mean dogs tethered to his cart to keep others from stealing his stuff, and to guard him at night while he slept. I don't like dogs, but considered doing the same, as turf wars for sleeping spots and recyclables could get ugly. To avoid confrontations, I roamed areas outside the central business districts, or got up early to raid trash cans in tourist meccas. Most of the street warriors slept late or stayed drunk all day, and were inconsistent in their quests for survival.

Anyway, Archie needed a friend and said he would provide nighttime protection if we slept close to each other (platonically, of course) and shared a few beers or a meal. I reluctantly agreed, and soon found that we got along well enough, even though he seldom bathed and had virtually no education. He was streetwise, though, and showed me sleeping spots where no one would bother us, and taught me to pick girlie magazines from the trash, then sell them to adult book stores.

His dogs seldom barked, but bit instead. We were wakened several times when someone who was trying to steal from our carts in the middle of the night yelped with pain and burst out cursing. The dogs bit hard and usually left good-sized puncture marks. Each morning we would go separate ways and meet up later at the recycling center. There were times, though, that we rolled along together and brought in a huge haul to split. I could tell you about numerous moments and adventures, but one Thanksgiving sticks in my mind.

It had rained. Our things were wet, and my blankets were soaked. I woke up shivering with cold. I was about to break camp and head for a laundromat to dry them, when an Asian man walked up to us and said he was going to a nearby Vietnamese restaurant and put a hundred dollars on a tab for us. We could go there and order anything we wanted for takeout within that budget. We did, and subsequently sat under a bridge with a hot, delicious feast.

Archie's dogs were regularly given treats by people. We were handed leftovers from fancy restaurants by tourists, but the kindness of that man moved me to tears. Eggrolls, soup, rice, spicy pork, teriyaki chicken and steamed cabbage. I relished each bite and felt better about my ability to survive my ordeal.

One day I got offered a job at the recycling center. This led to a room in a pay-by-the-week hotel and my subsequent reinstatement into the realm of self-sufficiency. My body healed to a reasonable degree, and I have worked hard ever since. I lost track of Archie for a while, but heard that he'd been hit by a car and badly injured. When I did see him again I was appalled by his condition. The dogs had been euthanized, since no one but Archie could keep them from attacking strangers. Archie was housed in a state-run rehab facility, where he would ultimately die of pneumonia. That day, though, we sat on a bench outside the place and shared a quart of beer and a paper bag lunch. I'd brought two plastic cups, and Archie sipped his slowly, while we talked and watched the flow of pedestrian traffic. We shook hands as brothers afterwards, and I never saw him again.

Just Stories
By Howard Schneider

"Zulka! Where are you?"

"The kitchen. Where else?"

" I need to talk to you," Zulka's husband said as he charged through the door, out of breath from running up three floors of stairs of their apartment building.

"What? Suddenly you have to tell me when you need to talk to me?"

"This is different."

"What's so different?'

"I'm a murderer."

"A murderer? Morris, what have you done?"

"My stories. They're coming true. People are dying, and it's my fault."

"I'll make coffee. Then tell me what craziness you're thinking. Sit, calm down," Zulka said, pulling a chair out from her kitchen work table. She cleared a space on the cluttered surface, took the lid off a tin containing fresh-made cake, then started a pot of coffee.

"With milk," Morris said as Zulka poured the steaming brew into a cup in front of him.

"For thirty-six years you've been having milk. You think I don't know?"

They sat in silence for a while, taking occasional sips of coffee, waiting for the right moment. Finally, Morris said, "The endings of my stories, they're happening in real life. I read it in the newspapers. Even on the radio I hear about it."

"That's impossible, Morris. You write fiction. Real life it's not."

"That's what I always thought. But now what's happening is the same as in my stories."

"Like what?"

"Last week. The woman who fell onto the track at the Ninth Avenue Station and was killed by the train to Coney Island. That was in my *A Bad Hand* story published in Writers' Magazine last year."

"That was coincidence. Accidents like that happen all the time. You're being paranoid."

"That's only one example. There's more."

"There's more?"

"There's more."

"What more?"

"Remember my story two years ago about the anthropologist who went to the Amazon to study that remote tribe?"

"No, I don't remember. What about it?"

"It was in the news today. He was killed the same way I wrote how the cannibals he was studying had him for dinner. And that's not all!"

"Morris! Calm down. That tribe didn't read your story. It's just another coincidence."

"I'm telling you. There's more. Like you wouldn't believe."

"What?"

"That short story I sold to 'Weird Tales' last month. The one when the woman in Florida was eaten by a gigantic alligator that came into her apartment because she left the back door open so her dog could go in and out. Remember? How her mother-in-law told her how stupid she was to do that. It was on the internet today. Exactly the same! They found her remains in the alligator's stomach. They did DNA analysis, for Christ sake."

"What? The alligator read your story? You think it subscribes to that magazine? I don't think so. Morris! Get hold of yourself. You're overreacting."

"Overreacting? You don't know the half of it. Something's going on. And it's not good. One thing I know. God is going to punish me. Just wait! You'll see."

"If God was so concerned about your stories, she wouldn't have let these terrible things happen in the first place," Zulka said, with the authority of a rabbi explaining a passage from the Torah.

"She? What's with the 'She'? You think God is a woman?"

"Morris! That's not the point. The point is that you're getting carried away with your paranoia. Your stories can't control what happens in the world. You write fiction. The world is real. There's no connection. Think how many stories you've written that didn't have any consequences in real life. Please. Don't let events that are nothing more than simple coincidence make you think your writing can affect human events. After all, you're not God."

Morris poured more coffee into his cup and took another piece of Zulka's almond pound cake. After a while, in a calmer manner, he said, "Maybe you're right. There are a lot of stories I've published that haven't come true, even though they had what might be considered upsetting endings."

"That's right, Morris. Like the one you wrote a few months ago. The one about an apartment building going up in flames with all those people trapped inside. The one in which the drug dealers lived on the top floor?"

"Yeah. I got $500 for that one. I knocked it out in two days."

"That'll come in handy, too. It'll pay for the electrical problem we need to get fixed. Should I make another pot of coffee?" Zulka asked, as she got up from the table and went over to the sink. "I'll open this window a little. It's getting kind of smoky in here, don't you think?"

Now Where Is She?
By Howard Schneider

Barney Klagger rushed from room to room looking for his wife Hilda. She was nowhere to be found.

"God damn it, Hilda! Where are you?" Barney's frustration was building. "There's someone here wants to see you. She's waiting in the front room."

Barney went to the basement and searched everywhere; the remodeled rec room, the laundry room, the furnace room, even the pantry where Hilda stored all the canned vegetables and fruit she put up each year.

No Hilda.

"Maybe she went to the back yard," he mumbled as he clomped back up the stairs. "Or maybe up to her sewing room. I'll check there first. Damn that woman."

In the hallway, he opened the door to the stairwell that went upstairs, but instead encountered coats and raingear arranged neatly on a row of wooden hangers, as well as an assortment of boots and shoes on the floor. He slammed the door shut and shifted over to the one next to it. He opened that one, stood staring at the stairs for a second, then started climbing.

"You up here?" he cried when he reached the landing.

Again, no Hilda.

Back downstairs, he went through the kitchen and out onto the rear porch.

"Damn that woman!" he repeated. He stood on the porch steps and scanned the yard, seeing the turned-under garden, a row of azaleas along the cedar fence, and the freshly painted side of the garage.

But no Hilda.

"Hilda?" he yelled.

No reply.

He went inside and made his way to the living room.

"She must have gone out front," he said to himself.

He glanced at the woman sitting on the sofa flipping through a magazine, then opened and stepped through the door. Standing on the stoop, he looked around their little patch of grass, then up and down the street.

"Hilda?"

No answer.

He went back inside.

"Damn that woman!"

The woman on the sofa looked up, then laid the magazine aside. She reached for a tiny device lying on the coffee table in front of her. She inserted it into her ear, then said, "Barney! What are you doing?"

"Who are you?" Barney asked, a puzzled look on his unshaven face.

"Barney, honey. I'm your wife. Hilda."

Barney didn't say anything. He just stood there looking at her.

Hilda picked up the magazine off the sofa cushion and laid it on the table, then rose to her feet and went to where Barney stood at the still-open door.

"How about a cup of tea? We'll make your favorite kind." She shut the door, then took Barney's trembling hand firmly in hers and led him into the kitchen.

Dinner at the Top of the World
By Mizeta Moon

It was my girlfriend's idea to take a train from northern India to Lhasa, Tibet. I kept telling her that the high altitude would make my breathing problems worse, and that I'd rather take a boat tour down the Ganges. She was one of those Type-A personalities, however, and thought I was being a whiny party pooper. In the end, we slept on the floor of a crowded rail car towed behind a wheezing steam locomotive and arrived in Lhasa on the fourteenth of May. Checking into a modestly priced hotel, we were informed that the next day was special, as it was the incense festival where prowling ghosts would be driven away by thousands of dressed-up people partying in the streets.

I had already had my fill of temples, monasteries and clouds of incense in India. Being a non-believer in any form of god or religion, my only interest had been the beautiful topography that part of the world had to offer. My field of study is architecture, and the juxtaposition of beautiful buildings and incredible natural surroundings was inspiring me to go back to America and construct something wonderful. Lhasa seemed to be the center of yet more religious fervor. The constant ringing of bells and clanging of gongs gave me a headache within hours of arrival.

My girlfriend was out on the streets at the crack of dawn, cell phone in hand and camera at the ready. I slept in as long as I could, then met her for lunch in the hotel's dining room. Reading the menu was a challenge, so I finally settled for some butter-laden tea and bread with goat cheese. I have to admit that it wasn't all that bad.

"I have a surprise for you," she said, as we stepped into crowded streets filled with noise and revelry. My chest felt like an elephant was sitting on it and breathing was difficult. I knew she would hassle me if I went back to the room and lay down, so I feigned interest in her announcement.

Oh . . . I forgot to tell you that my girlfriend's father was a United States senator, and she and I were roughing it as a rite of passage, so what came next was par for the course.

"My father arranged for us to attend a dinner party where the Dalai Lama will be the honored guest. Not first table of course, but close enough to see his eminence without obstruction. Isn't that exciting?"

Ho hum. Another bald dude in a robe. They were ubiquitous everywhere we'd been lately. "Wow! That's great," I said, knowing any other response would mean no sex for weeks.

The dinner party turned out pretty good. I was thankful to be in a relatively quiet hall with only a hundred or so people instead of on the streets of Lhasa where the noise was deafening. If those ghosts were still hanging around, I would be surprised.

Roasted and ground barley known as tsampa was heavily featured. Noodles of various shapes were made from it and then steeped in broths known as thukpa when veggies and bits of yak or goat meat were added. There was also this thing called sha phaley, which was meat and cabbage in bread. An assortment of cheeses and butters were strange flavors for my palate, but weren't unpleasant. My biggest problem was eating with bamboo chopsticks. Everything kept sliding off and I finally resorted to using my fingers, as no silverware was provided. I nearly choked when I slathered a hunk of mutton with a hot sauce called sepen that brought tears to my eyes.

The whole time I kept wishing that I was scarfing a McDonald's double cheeseburger with a side of fries and a cold beer.

When the bald dude got up and started blessing everyone, I asked where the bathroom was and left my girlfriend to her moment of glory. I knew she would brag about it forever, so thoughts of ending our relationship popped back into my mind. Hopefully, we could finish our trip and fly home from Bangkok before she became aware of my plans to defect. I have to say, though, that I slept well that night. My last bottle of whiskey that I'd purchased at the duty-free store in Amsterdam before flying to India went down smoothly and drowned out the revelry.

Santa's Beer Sleigh
By Mizeta Moon

When it's nearly freezing and you're living outside, beer would not be most people's drink of choice. Most folks would dream of cocoa, or hot toddies by a roaring fire. A bunch of us were huddled on the loading dock of an abandoned warehouse, and all we could talk about was booze.

Three Finger Frank had a skinny joint, but it didn't make it all the way around. Chicago Pete had two packs of smokes, so we all got one as a Christmas present from a guy that would usually bite your head off if you asked. None of us had any money, so a trip to the corner store for a bottle of wine was out of the question. It seemed like we were destined to sleep with dreams of lager running through our heads. I looked out at the brightly-lit city and envisioned cocktail parties with cheese plates, finger foods and leftovers taken home that would die in the fridge. Sighing, I pulled my blanket tighter and took one last puff of my free smoke before lying down on the concrete.

Suddenly, there was a racket that made us all sit bolt upright. Flashing lights were approaching in the sky and I thought we were about to become victims of an airplane crash. Instead, our Christmas wish was about to come true.

With a thud, this huge sleigh landed right in front of the warehouse. There were no reindeer, but there was a fat guy in a red suit. The sleigh had been welded to the cab of a Peterbilt, whose diesel sent echoes bouncing off nearby walls. I stared in amazement at rows of beer kegs lining both sides of the sleigh. Glistening taps promised to deliver frothy manna to those dying of thirst.

After the fat guy shut down the rig, he handed out souvenir mugs from several different breweries to each of us. Then came the test.

"If you've been naughty, no suds will flow, and you'll walk away in woe," he said.

"If you've been nice, you can come twice, and fill your glass to the brim. Grasp the handle of your favorite brew, and we'll see what Santa has for you."

Nervously, I approached the tap advertising a local craft beer. I couldn't shake the memory of pushing that old crippled lady out of line at the soup kitchen. Would that disqualify me? What about . . .? Hell, the list was really long. Sure enough, while others quaffed their suds, my glass stood empty and dry. I shuffled away despondently, and hoped I could drown out the sounds of revelry to get some sleep.

"Have you learned your lesson?" a musical, child-like voice inquired from behind me.

Turning around, I discovered a gamine woman in a semi-transparent silver dress standing on the sidewalk. Once I'd recovered my wits, she would explain to me how one always has chances to be naughty or nice. And that choices we make determine our punishment or reward.

"Would you like a beer?" she asked sweetly, after citing how badly I'd failed. How those banded together by poverty and displacement should be even more charitable.

"Please. Yes! I would really like a beer."

"Then you may have one, but not two. That will come next year if you promise to try harder."

I swore to change my ways right there on the spot. Never did a beer taste so good.

When the gamine woman and the fat guy flew off in the Peterbilt, we raised our mugs to the sky. Surprise, surprise, Chicago Pete handed out another round of smokes. I pulled my blanket close and sat puffing on mine, hoping that old lady would be in the soup line the next day, and I could apologize.

Reading in the Park
By Howard Schneider

Her one-room apartment was stifling hot, and noise from early-evening-commute traffic flooding in through the open window was unbearable. Finally, she grabbed her purse and the library book she was halfway through, went down one floor to the street and headed to a little park at the end of her block. She found a vacant bench in the shade of an old maple and settled in for a few hours of reading.

When the light became too dim to read, she closed the book and prepared to leave. But just as she got up and started to walk away, a big man came up behind her and shoved her back down onto the bench. She cried out when her elbow smashed into the arm rest. The book fell to the ground.

"Give me your purse, lady," the man said.

"Tim! What the hell are you doing?" another man yelled as he ran up to the one who had accosted the woman.

The woman sat still, clutched her purse close to her chest, and remained silent, as if too afraid to say anything or scream for help.

"Come on, man. We're not so desperate we need to rob an old woman," the newcomer said.

"The hell we ain't. We haven't had a thing to eat all day. What else are we supposed to do? Pray for a miracle?"

"I'm hungry too, but I don't like the idea of stealing from old people. Or anybody else, for that matter."

"That shelter we tried was full. It was turning people away. We can't go back there. Are we gonna have to dig through garbage cans?"

"If we have to, yes. But we're not gonna take this woman's money. We're not thieves. Homeless bums maybe, but not thieves."

They continued arguing for a while, both adamant about their intentions. The woman didn't move, just sat clutching her purse and looking back and forth between the two men.

Finally, the big man who had demanded the woman's purse walked off shaking his head and swearing vociferously.

The man who remained looked at the woman apologetically for a brief moment, then turned and followed his companion.

"Wait," the woman said. She opened her purse and took out a worn billfold. She opened the billfold and removed six one-dollar-bills, then held them out to the man.

"Here. This is all I have. Take it and buy some food. There's a little market on the corner."

The man looked at the money, then stepped closer. He carefully withdrew four of the bills from her hand and put them in his pocket.

"This will do," he said. "Thank you." He then turned and took off running to catch up with his friend.

The woman reached down and retrieved the book from where it lay in the dirt, then rose to her feet and went back to her apartment.

Eager to Serve/The Zealous Juror
By Mizeta Moon

Man! I hope I get selected for a good one. Not some penny-ante shoplifting case. I mean like a juicy, grizzly murder with lots of gory crime scene photos.

Look at some of these bozos, waiting to see if they get called and hoping they don't. Old farts, punkers, purple hair, no hair, most of them would rather be anywhere but here. Not me! When my summons came I jumped for joy.

I was first in line and made sure I got a good seat. Watching everyone reluctantly file in, I could see that a real cross-section of humanity was represented, but none of them shared my passion to punish some crook.

The yoga-loving health food freak.

The half-awake trashy barmaid.

Several irritated executive types.

Bored housewives galore.

Computer addicts that couldn't wait to plug in.

Cell phone game players.

Coffee baristas and millennial hipsters, all avoiding personal contact, wrapped in a cocoon of silence.

First call out . . . Damn! Didn't get to go. Oh well. There's a whole day ahead.

Gotta remember not to act so eager this time if I get called for screening. Last time I really wanted to fry that drunk that ran over an old lady in a crosswalk. Should have just answered questions and not blurted out stuff.

WOW! Check out that hot blonde. I'd sure like to get sequestered with her.

Uh oh. Mr. B.O., don't sit next to me or I'll whip out some of my scented hand sanitizer and rub it on you.

Wish they would show a good movie and serve popcorn. Cheapass justice department. Guess they like keeping us catatonic.

Boo. Got called up for a boring civil case. Stereotype lawyers. Young buck representing a rich guy plaintiff. Clean-cut old guy and a tight-ass woman for the accused. So solemn, officious. Bet the woman knows how to boogie outside of court, but the old guy looks like someone who frowns in their sleep.

Who me? I'm excused? Bummer deal. Ha, ha.

Back to the jury room. Hopefully, all the spicy trials haven't been empaneled while I was gone.

Seems like there's always a loud mouth. Acting important. Full of crap. Bad language. Bad attitude. In a room full of strangers, showing more of himself than anyone cares to see. Man! Hurry up! Call my name again.

What if I don't get to see some blood and guts? Or listen to a bunch of whiny butts leak tears all over the courtroom? It'll be two years before they summon me again. Why can't being on juries be my job? I'd be good at convicting people.

Lunch already? I'm not hungry for anything but some action.

Maybe Judge Judy will make a celebrity appearance. I'd love to see her whack some asshole with her gavel.

The bathrooms are sure busy. I guess it's true that most people are full of shit.

Look at that freak! Dude . . . Get a life and a haircut. You'd certainly scare the crap out of criminals if you got chosen.

Tick tock, tick tock, stop the clock, I'm running out of time.

Please! Start naming names. Everyone is numb, sleeping, bored. I am foaming at the mouth.

Damn! Next call out and I didn't make it.

Break time. Smokers run for it. Check out, check in. Get scanned by suspicious-eyed sheriffs. All for a puff or two.

Oh goody! Got called for a sex crime case with a laundry list of charges. Not murder, but maybe there'll be good details.

Me! Me! Pick me. I am eager to serve.

It's About Norman A. Ziglinski
By Howard Schneider

Good evening, Radio of America listeners. I'm Helen Henderson, host for tonight's episode of our Interviews for the Arts series. This evening I welcome none other than Catherine McAdams, one of Chicago's most esteemed musicians. Catherine is first chair violin of our world-class symphony orchestra, and a teacher and composer with too many awards, recordings and other accomplishments to list in the short time we have today.

Hello, Ms. McAdams. Welcome to the program.

Thank you, Helen. I'm thrilled to be here.

Let's start with your background in music. What were the key factors that brought your musical genius to fruition?

Oh, my goodness, Helen. That's a bit of an overstatement. I'm certainly no genius. Like many of my colleagues, I majored in music at college, then studied at Julliard. However, as for early influences, the most important factor was encouragement from a next-door neighbor.

Oh? Who was that?

He was an immigrant from Eastern Europe. He came here in the mid-1930s. He didn't like to talk about his past, although he did mention something about being one of the lucky ones that got out.

He was a nice old gentleman, polite, kind, always telling me how beautiful my playing was, and that I must learn scales, and practice. Most of all, he told me not to become discouraged. He gave me the gentle encouragement that's so important to a child. His name was Mr. Ziglinski; Norman A. Ziglinski. He passed away when I was a senior in high school.

Were your parents as supportive of your music?

No . . . .. My father died when I was a baby. During my childhood, my mother was either at her waitressing job or drinking in front of the TV. I don't think she cared one way or the other what I did, although she did give me a plastic ukulele for my sixth birthday. I remember it had a decal of a hula dancer on it. It was only present she ever gave me. I'll always be grateful that she did.

Was that ukulele the beginning of your musical development?

It certainly was. One day Mr. Ziglinski heard me plunking away tunelessly on our front porch and came over to listen. For some reason, he took an interest, and within a few minutes had taught me the chords and strumming pattern for Five Foot Two, a song that was quite popular then. Over the following week, he showed me all kinds of chord fingering positions and strumming patterns. In no time at all I was able to play along with songs on the radio. It came easy to me, and I played pretty much every day. Later, he told me I had perfect pitch and should take up the violin. He said it would be a waste of a God-given gift if I didn't.

Was your neighbor a musician?

He certainly was! An accomplished violinist. He said he played in orchestras in Europe before he came to America, but hadn't been able to get into one here because of limited funds for orchestras and so much competition. Instead, he worked in a shoe store downtown until he retired. But he still played his violin most evenings. I still remember the hauntingly sad strains flowing out the window of a first-floor room he rented in the house next to ours. I've never heard anything like those pieces since. They must have been his own compositions. Nobody ever complained about his music because it was so beautiful. When he eventually stopped playing it was like losing a part of my soul.

That is a wonderful story. Thank you for sharing it with our audience. How old were you when you got your first violin?

I was eleven when Mr. Ziglinski gave me his own instrument. It was quite old and had beautiful rich tones. He told me that his hands were so arthritic he couldn't play anymore. He said that it shouldn't go unplayed. That's when he started giving me weekly lessons for free. His other students had to pay. But not me. He knew I couldn't afford them. I saw him for an hour lesson every week until just before he died. I still have his violin; it's the one I play every day.

Unfortunately, we're about out of time and haven't talked about your amazing career yet. What's next for you?

As far as the coming year, it's really just more of the same. Music, music, music. But I'd like to correct you about not delving into my career during our conversation. That's exactly what we've talked about. There wouldn't have been a music career for me if it hadn't been for Mr. Ziglinski. His willingness to share his knowledge and invest his time inspired me to do the best I could. He and he alone made me what I am today, and every time I place his violin under my chin and prepare to play, I ask myself how would it sound to him? Would I earn his approval?

How fortunate you were that such a caring individual came into your life. Thank you, Catherine, for being with us today.

It was my pleasure. Thank you for having me.

Deaf Bartender
By Mizeta Moon

Lavinia didn't mind working in a heavy metal club where volume was always max and drink orders were yelled to servers by partying patrons. Her handicap made her perfect for the job. She was always focused, and never got swept up in the excitement. She could feel music as a physical presence, but didn't soar with it, like hundreds of stoned out, drunken revelers that were in the club night after night. She was there to work, and her goal was making money. Her form of madness was shopping for shoes and handbags.

Lavinia placed her magnetic order board on the bar at the beginning of each shift, along with a sign that said, **The Bartender Is Deaf.** Patrons often took it as a joke and laughed. If people didn't appreciate the fact that she was totally deaf, well, what could she do? She was halfway decent at reading lips, but if one followed simple instructions, and placed a marker by type of liquor, number of drinks, etc. she could crank them out like nobody's business.

Her menu board was extensive. She knew thousands of drinks by memory, and could deal with even off-the-wall concoctions. Lavinia was nothing if not professional.

Her biggest weakness was this guy. He started out mowing her lawn, but had crept into her bed one night and never left. He became a habit somehow, and even though she knew he was worthless, kept him in cigarettes and beer, while he kept promising to paint the kitchen. Would this be the night she sent him away?

In the middle of her shift, Lavinia looked up from digging in the ice bin and saw someone she would love to be with walk in. Her blood surged, as it had when she'd seen them several times before. She asked herself why she hadn't just bit this person's neck like a vampire and made them her own.

Starting to make their favorite cocktail, Lavinia wondered if she was looking good, and smelled okay after cleaning the beer cooler. Was her breath sweet? Was her smile over the top? Would they stay a while and talk to her in sign language? She loved the fact they could speak fluently with their hands and didn't need to use the menu board. Just then, her bubble burst and the smile retreated from her face. Standing by the door was Mr. Worthless, looking like he needed another handout.

Besides her menu, Lavinia kept a dry-erase board handy in order to talk when necessary. She could speak quite a few words, but the softness of her voice and slurred enunciation made it impossible to understand her over the din of the club. When Mr. Worthless sidled up to the bar, wearing the grin she once found endearing, she printed, **what now**? in capital letters, using three exclamation points and two question marks.

Grabbing the pen, he wrote, "The guys are coming over to watch TV, and we're out of beer. I sorta promised pizza, too." Lavinia now fully understood that she had adopted an untrainable dog that would chew your slippers, pee in the house, then wag its tail while begging for a tasty bone. Looking over his shoulder, she saw her heartthrob leave a few bills on the bar, then sign "thank you" as he melted into the crowd.

Infuriated, Lavinia reached into her tip jar, pulled out a twenty, and then crumpled it into a ball. Tossing it into his face, she grabbed the board, and wrote, **"I'm busy. Go away. Never bother me at work again."** In the background, people were waving for attention and her menu board was filled with orders. One of the servers glared at her maliciously for the slow-down in service.

For the next half-hour, she worked frenetically, playing catch up. Angered patrons left skimpy tips while her armpits and forehead dripped with sweat. To top it all off, she really needed a bathroom break, but her floor manager was busy yelling at a punker who'd violated club rules and lit a joint inside. Didn't he know about the smoke circle behind the dumpster? Finally unable to wait any longer, she stepped out from behind the bar and grabbed Darlene by the shoulder.

Darlene was a big breasted bubblehead who had been a bartender once, but preferred to hustle drinks on the floor and show off her cleavage. Shoving Darlene's protesting form behind the bar, and indicating her desperate need to pee, Lavinia fought her way through the mosh pit, cut ahead of a pink-haired tattooed woman, and dived into a stall. The woman yelled curses, but Lavinia never heard a word.

By the time she got back behind the bar, Darlene had managed to pour two beers and was flirting with a member of the opening band. The menu board looked like a Rubik's cube and people stood three deep at the bar. The floor manager finally came to her rescue, but she remained swamped the rest of the night.

Saddened by the turn of events, Lavinia emptied her tip jar, cleaned her station, and then put on her coat for the walk home. She planned to throw out anyone she found sleeping on her couch, and to tell Mr. Worthless that the locks would be changed. He could go back to mowing lawns.

Almost in tears, she stepped into the night. Fog in the air was appropriate for her state of mind. Her legs ached, her back hurt and part of her wanted to lie down and die.

She didn't notice the man standing on the sidewalk until he stepped in front of her, smiled, and signed, "Would you like to join me for breakfast?"

"You've got quite a smile on your face," the floor manager wrote on the dry-erase board when Lavinia came on shift. "Did you get laid? I know you were in a shitty mood when you left last night."

Lavinia turned the board around, cleared it after reading, and then wrote, "None of your business. Thanks for helping me out towards the end. That won't happen again."

"No problem. Gonna be busy again tonight. The Ass Bangers are playing. Their single went viral online. Don't like 'em myself; hate *singers* who growl, but they'll sell a ton of drinks. Want backup?"

"No. Just make sure I get a pee break without having to run for it."

The floor manager smiled sheepishly, then walked away. Hopefully, no assholes would make her go apeshit tonight, and leave other duties unattended.

It was always quiet when Lavinia first came on. While she checked stock, chilled glasses, cut limes and prepped her station, she thought about the turnaround that occurred in predawn.

Stepping into a virtual stranger's car was frightening for a moment. "What if he's a serial killer, and you're some dumbass hoping to fall in love? Just because he's cute, that doesn't make him safe." She ignored her internal natterings and settled into a comfortable seat. He had a cool car. She had no idea what it was, but the heater worked. Wherever they were going didn't matter. Everything felt right.

She was concerned about their safety when he kept taking his hands off the wheel to fully introduce himself, but somehow, they got to their destination. It wasn't a restaurant, as she'd expected. It was his home. The garage door opened when his car approached, and Lavinia wondered if she should bail. Her smile would not be so bright if she had.

He made breakfast. He was polite. It turned out he had a job. There were no ex-wives, or adult children to thwart supplicants to daddy's wallet. Even if there were some, Lavinia wouldn't begrudge their sleeping on the couch instead of getting a job and renting an apartment. After all, she'd allowed it for months. But! That was in the past and she was thinking way too far ahead.

The locksmith only charged her fifty bucks to change all the locks. Mr. Worthless took his toothbrush and ran. Even though she couldn't speak very well, Lavinia could screech and throw a hellacious tantrum.

Her new-found friend (hopefully boyfriend), talked to her about books he'd read. Showed her his collection of antique shrimp cocktail forks, and regaled her with anecdotes. Tired, but thankful for the reprieve from drudgery, she'd finally asked for a ride home, and was immediately indulged. It was nice to meet a man who respected women.

Orders were beginning to trickle in. Time to focus on the job. She'd read about the Ass Bangers in *Rolling Stone*. They usually threw dildos to the audience. If things went right, she wouldn't need one ever again.

Three women in leathers strode up to the bar and plunked down orders for Sex on the Beach. Were they dreaming? Or was she?

For the next three nights, Lavinia kept looking towards the door, but he never showed. They hadn't exchanged numbers, or email addresses, so she had no way to tell him how much she wanted to see him again. She blew a few drink orders, which led to a bitching out from the floor manager, but after she accepted the fact he was not in attendance, she knuckled down, and made a shit-pot full of tips for her days off.

Filled with overactive hormonal longings, and increasingly louder whispers of rejection, she tempered her emotional turmoil by going shopping. Taking a cab home from Nordstrom's afterwards, she sat amid a pile of packages that contained seven new purses and eleven pairs of shoes. Not to mention two sets of pajamas, several shades of nylons and a two-hundred-dollar perfume. How the saleswoman talked her into that, she'd never know. Was she horny or what? Ridiculous, she told herself. How could any man create such a disturbance in her life?

Walking around her apartment, wearing nothing but panties and new shoes, she asked herself if any man was worth giving up one's freedom for. Was she willing to jump from a loser to someone who looked like a winner, but could be gay, bisexual (how did she feel about that?), or simply an illusion? Was he emotionally available? Was she grasping at straws because Mr. Worthless drained her reservoir of indulgence? What was happiness, really? A glass of wine?

Watching a magnificent sunset? A sweaty encounter in a filthy alley? Perhaps a bowl of ice-cream with a high school sweetheart? She was filled with questions, but devoid of answers.

When she walked into the club to start her next shift, she was despondent. How had puppy love put her in such a funk? After all, the guy made no moves on her, nor had he professed undying love and admiration. He'd simply cooked her an excellent breakfast, talked fluently with his hands, and made her want to feel them massaging her back. Did that make her needful? Was he staying away because he could feel her desire to be desired?

When she found him sitting at the bar, swirling ice around in his glass with a straw, her heart nearly burst out of her chest. Her underarms immediately flooded, and she almost peed herself. OMG! Was she smitten, or what? She fought down the urge to have her hands fly through the air like little hummingbirds, to question his whereabouts over the last few days. She held no claim on his time, nor any right to do so. Instead, she pointed at his glass with a questioning look, and then signed, "Hi. Nice to see you."

After pushing his glass forward for a refill, he signed, "I hope you don't mind that I'm here so early. The floor manager is an old friend. She let me in when I told her I wanted to talk to you before the madness starts."

Oh! What did he want to talk about?

While Lavinia did side work and made sure she was ready for the onslaught, he told her that his cousin had been killed in a car crash several hours after he'd taken her home. He'd flown out that evening to comfort the family, and had just returned. Lavinia nearly cut her trembling finger while she resisted the desire to wrap her arms around him and soothe pain that was obvious in his eyes. Why was she holding back? Their chemistry was so strong it hung in the air like a swarm of highly-charged atoms.

"What I wanted to talk about is whether you'd be willing to spend your next off time in Bend with me? I know it's a lot to ask when we hardly know each other, but I would love having you there while I pull myself together. I've taken a short leave of absence from work because my cousin and I were very close."

"Why Bend?"

"I own a cabin outside of town. There are great hiking trails that can help bring one's thoughts back in focus. Oh ... if you don't like that sort of stuff, there are plenty of fun things to do around town, as well as beautiful byways to explore by car."

Should she play hard to get? Going out of town with someone and being without transportation if things went poorly ...

"I'm not off for five days. That's a long time to wait."

"I'll do some yardwork and paint my fence. The reward of your company at the end will make time fly. What do you say?"

Her smile was as dazzling as sun breaking over mountains in the morning. Her hands shook so badly, she could barely speak.

"Will I need a heavy coat?"

The club was filling with partiers ready to rumble. Drink orders arrived, so he said goodbye and left. The floor manager walked up with a big grin on her face. "So! You caught a good one. Don't screw it up. If you hurt him, I'll be very angry. We've been friends for years," she wrote on the dry-erase board. Seeing Lavinia's questioning look, she continued. "No. Not that kind of friends. There's a reason why, but I'll let him tell you. Now get to work and keep your head out of your ass."

"I wasn't circumcised as a baby. My parents waited until I was twelve to have it done."

They were in his cabin with a fire blazing, even though it was not overly cold. Its ambiance drew them closer together on the couch. After a day of tramping through woods, splashing through streams, and watching a magnificent sunset, they'd eaten a delicious meal he prepared, and now sipped wine slowly while conversing.

"The operation went poorly, and I developed a massive infection that forced the doctors to remove my testicles. The reason your floor manager, Elsa, and I never became an item is that she wanted babies. I don't know how well you know her, but her kids are cool. I've known them since birth. Her husband and I fish together each fall. We go out for pizza from time to time, or take in a ballgame. Anyway, there was no point in getting started on a journey we couldn't complete."

Lavinia was blown away. She'd never heard of such a thing. It was certainly not what she'd expected. At least he wasn't telling her he was in love with some guy named Armand. How did she feel now? The attraction was still there. She'd wanted to kiss him all day, but now understood why he'd hung back. It was nice that he had no plan to delude her. After a long pause, and a few sips of wine, she snuggled into him and asked, "Can you perform at all?"

He grimaced sadly, took a big gulp of wine, and said, "No. My little unit is strictly for emptying my bladder. All I can offer is cuddling and kissing, the attention of my lips and hands. There's room in my heart for you if you care to move in. I think you're the most wonderful woman I've ever met, and it would make me proud to walk down any street in the world holding your hand. Maybe I'm saying too much, but I keep feeling that you want me too."

"I do," she replied. "It's just that ... this is a surprise. Can we sit here for a while and not talk? Now that I've found you, I don't want to walk away, unless I discover that I have the same needs as Elsa."

He opened a fresh bottle of cabernet, then stoked the fire and placed her hiking boots on the hearth to dry. She wrapped herself cocoon-like in her own arms and appeared to fall asleep. Nearly two hours passed and he prepared himself for yet another rejection.

He was washing dishes when Lavinia came up behind him, turned him round, then kissed him full on the mouth. Cuddling was good enough. Lips, hands and tongues could deliver pleasure. If she ever felt the need for penetration, then it was probably a good thing that one of the dildos tossed into the crowd by the Ass Bangers landed behind the bar.

The Horror
By Howard Schneider

An overly loud doorbell roused me from a near-stupor, and out of the easy chair in front of the muted television with its panel of voiceless blabbers struggling for the attention of an uncaring camera. A silent mantel clock showed 5:47. Through the front window a misty dimness struggling through a low layer of rain clouds confirmed the clock's truth.

Somebody's here. Half-awake, I stumbled out of the room and down the hall to the front door.

Through the glass pane I spied an old man dressed in black. Rivulets of rainwater streamed from the wide brim of a hat that looked like one a Quaker, or maybe a rabbi or priest, would have worn in some far-distant past. I didn't like the look of him—scary on first sight. It wasn't his full white beard or large frame. No! It was the intensity of his clear blue eyes. Their menacing clarity radiated power. *Or was it determination?*

He could see me looking out at him, maybe even sense my hesitation to open the door. He leaned forward to thrust his face closer to the glass separating us. The heat of his stare startled me, but seemed to command me to turn the door knob. And I did.

Without waiting for an invitation, he pushed his way in, brushed me aside, and marched straight down the hall into the living room.

"Hey! What are you doing? I don't want you in here!" I yelled, as I followed him. He stopped in the middle of the room and turned to face me. He towered over me, even taller than I first perceived. *How could someone so old look so strong?* I wondered.

His voice was like a soft growl, deep, resonant, but not loud. "I've found you. Twenty-eight years it's taken. But here I am. And there you are."

I took a step back, wanting to get away, but was afraid to run.

"Who are you? What do you want?"

"Look at me! Think! Think thirty years ago, to the time you destroyed my life, and all that I cherished!"

"Oh, my God! Is it you? How can this be! How did you find me?" My terror erupted in a rush of memory and pain. I took another step back, which he countered with a step forward, then another, coming so close I could feel his hot breath on my face. He leaned even closer; "I've come for revenge. To dispense long-delayed justice."

As he hovered in front me, the flash of memory lasted only an instant, but in that instant I envisioned the entire scene. The late-night hour; a red scooter leaning against a front yard tree: the hooded half-dozen locals who were neighbors, my father among them. All of them urging me, at an age ill-prepared to resist their goading, to toss the bottle of fluid with the lit wick through the window of the foreigner's house. I did, and we all ran into nearby woods from where we watched flames consume everything within their reach. But more than the vision, it is the screams of agony that haunt my dreams and fuel my remorse. Screams that dominate my being and can't be ignored.

He drew back a few paces and took a bottle of clear fluid from his coat pocket and unscrewed its lid. "Now, like my wife and children, you will experience the same cruel death you inflicted upon them."

The justice of his revenge was irrefutable. Back then, the fire had been determined to be accidental. That was the way of things at that time and in that place. But everyone knew, and eventually he learned what happened the night he was away. But before he learned the truth, I had already fled, perhaps because of shame for what I had done, as much as fear of retribution. I never returned or had contact with my family or anyone else in that town.

But even though my life had become nothing more than dreary existence waiting for the end, I wasn't ready to die yet. There was something I desperately needed to do. "Wait! Please. I beg you. Grant me one request."

"Why should I? I have no interest in any request of yours."

"Because it will help you, too," I replied, looking straight into his penetrating eyes.

He paused for a few seconds, then screwed the lid back on the bottle. "What do you mean?"

"I need you to forgive me. If you do, I will forgive you for what you are going to do. Isn't that a fair trade?" I stepped forward. He took several awkward steps back, as if he feared I had a contagious disease, and wanted to be out of range. "No one should have to go to their grave unforgiven, including you," I continued. "My gift of forgiveness will prevent your life turning into the kind of hell that mine has been. I owe you that."

Confusion flooded the aspect of his face that wasn't hidden by his beard. He shook his head back and forth, slowly, ponderously. After a long silence, he riveted his eyes on mine and said, "Forgiveness will change nothing. I have to do this, for the sake of my wife and children. You forfeited your right to exist by taking theirs. You understand, don't you? That I will do what I must."

I did understand, and accepted it. I also understood that the act of unspeakable horror I carried out those many years ago, which had damned me to lifelong remorse and sorrow, had at long last caught up with me. That the time to pay the steep price of justice had arrived. Yes, I accepted it, even welcomed it. *Finally, escape from the dreams.*

I took another step forward and held out my hand. "Will you forgive me?"

He hesitated a moment, then stepped forward and took my hand in his firm grip and said, "You are forgiven." Still holding my hand in his, he added, "Do you forgive me for what I am about to do?"

"Yes. I forgive you."

In silence, we stood for a long moment looking into each other's eyes. Then I released his hand and returned to my chair. I stared at a muted weatherman tracing the track of some far-off raging tempest on a world map as my executioner unscrewed the lid of the bottle.

A Blue Ribbon

By Howard Schneider

The girl and her friend paid the fifty-cent admission fee and headed directly to where food entries were being judged. Even though it was only mid-morning, it was already hot and humid, and they both worked up a sweat during the long walk from the fairgrounds entrance to their destination.

"I hope it's cooler in there," the girl said as they neared the big red-painted building.

'Me too," her friend said. "But mostly, I want to see if your cornbread won a ribbon. Everybody says it's real good. Even my grandma, and she makes cornbread every day, so she ought to know."

When they got inside, they went to a table where a lady answered people's questions and handed out lists of the food categories, different kinds of pamphlets, and information sheets. The lady said that cornbread was a category by itself, was judged the day before, and that they could find out the results from Mr. Grubbs, who was the judge for that category. The girls followed the lady's directions and found Mr. Grubbs in a far back corner where he was judging a vast assortment of cupcakes.

"Mr. Grubbs?"

"Yes?"

"I want to find out about my cornbread. If I got a ribbon," the girl said.

"What's your name?" he asked, as he withdrew a folded sheet of paper from his shirt pocket.

She told him and he moved his finger down a column of names until he came to hers. "Oh yeah, I remember your cornbread. Had kernels of colored corn in it, right?"

"Yes, sir. It did. Did I get a ribbon?"

"I'm sorry, but you didn't. There were 47 entries, so lots of competition, and a good number of excellent cornbreads, I might add. But don't give up. Try again next year."

"Did you eat all of my cornbread?" she asked.

"No. Of course not. I only taste a small sample. Why?"

"I'd like to have what you didn't need. We can have it for lunch."

"I'm sorry, but there's none left," he said, a sheepish look forming on his face.

"You said you tasted only a small piece. What happened to the rest?"

"My dog ate it. Every last bit of it," he said, nodding towards a big dog asleep under the table.

"What? How could that happen?"

"I was distracted by people wanting to know about the judging results. Millie, my yellow Lab, smelled and licked all the cornbreads at the end of the table where yours was displayed, then picked yours for *her* lunch. If she had been the judge, you'd have a ribbon." He chuckled a little, as if he had made a funny joke.

"Okay, if that's what happened, then I want a ribbon. A blue one," the girl said in no uncertain tone, in no way acknowledging his little joke.

"I can't give you a ribbon just because you want one. Or because my dog ate your cornbread," Mr. Grubbs said.

"You must have extra ones, don't you?" she asked. "I can't go home without a ribbon. Everybody would laugh at me. They already think I was foolish to enter in the first place."

Eventually her insistent pleas overcame his reluctance and he gave in. He went into a little locked room and returned shortly with a big blue ribbon. With a black marking pen, in neat block letters he wrote "Special Award" on the back.

The girl thanked the judge, gave Millie a scratch behind her ears, then turned to her friend and said, "Let's go see the chickens. They're in the next building."

When the two girls left the food building, they discovered that the temperature outside had become even higher. It was turning out to be a scorcher of a day, probably another record-breaker. And to make things worse, the chicken building was further away than the girl thought.

"My feet are on fire. It's this asphalt. It's so hot it's getting soft," the girl said to her friend as they made their way along treeless fairground walkways lacking even a hint of shade.

"It's those flimsy shoes you're wearing," her friend said, pointing at the girl's slipper-like red flats. "The heat from this steaming asphalt goes through those thin soles right into your feet. May as well be walking on hot coals. You should wear shoes like mine."

The girl glanced at her friend's sensible white running shoes and laughed. "You won't catch me wearing those things anywhere other than a soccer field. I'm perfectly willing to suffer a little in order to be fashionable. I wouldn't be seen in public wearing ugly clodhoppers like those."

"Well, they're your feet, but let's hurry. No need to overdo your suffering," her friend replied, as she increased her pace.

The two girls came through a door of the chicken building out of breath and nearly overcome by the scorching noon heat. After cooling down and adjusting their eyes to the darker environment, they noticed a patch of verdant green a few yards beyond the door. Upon closer inspection, they saw that it was a square of lush, perfectly manicured grass enclosed by a low split-rail fence. The girl with burning feet walked over to the exhibit, if that was what it was, and stared at it intently.

When her friend with the sensible shoes joined her, the girl with hot feet said, "I'm going to go in there. That grass looks so soft and cool, just what I need to take away this burning pain." She slipped out of her flimsy flats, and with one hand lifting up the bottom of her dress enough to clear the fence, and holding her blue ribbon in the other hand, stepped over the rail and onto the welcoming lawn. She slowly walked around the perimeter, then moved and stood in the middle, where she calmly luxuriated in the plush carpet of verdant green, sliding her feet back and forth as if she were massaging them.

"Maybe you better get out of there. What if —" the girl with sensible shoes started to say, but was suddenly interrupted by a shrill voice.

"What the Goddamn hell are you doing on my grass?" a skinny old man screamed as he came rushing across the chicken-house floor towards the two girls. A second later he came up to the split-rail fence, jostled the girl with the sensible shoes aside, and started yelling at the girl in the fenced-in area. "Get off my grass! You're damaging it. You're gonna destroy my work. Look what you've done. It's all torn up, and your foot prints are everywhere. How am I gonna win a blue ribbon after you messed it up so much?" It was obvious he was having a hard time restraining himself; he seemed to be on the verge of jumping over the fence and dragging the girl off his perfect little miniature lawn, but instead remained where he stood and screamed at the girl. "Get out of there! Get out of there!" he yelled . . . over and over, louder and louder each time.

The girl on the grass was stunned by the man's outburst and verbal attack. At first she couldn't understand what he was yelling about because of his near-hysterical demeanor. Then, as he continued, she came to understand that the patch of grass was his entry in what must be a landscape category, and that he was intent on winning a blue ribbon, and that he believed that the damage she had done, albeit minor, would result in him failing to be awarded that ribbon. But when she looked around the area and saw that there were no competing grass entries, she assumed that no matter what the condition of the lawn, as the only entry he would win by default. She further concluded that the old guy must be off his rocker, so she ignored his ranting and continued using his lawn as a massage device, twisting and turning to music playing inside her head.

Her disregard of his raving only further enraged the old man, propelling him into a state of frenzy. He ignored efforts of fair officials and other fair-goers to calm him, physically pushing them aside, even striking out at the more insistent ones. Finally, when he felt strong arms attempting to restrain him, he twisted to the side quickly, drew a pistol from a holster strapped around his waist and fired two bullets into the girl jumping around on his grass. She was dead before she landed on the soft lawn. The blue ribbon she had been holding so tightly while prancing and dancing on her bare feet was soon submerged in a spreading pool of her thick warm blood.

The old man walked off toward the chicken pens, waving his gun around at nobody in particular, and cackling manically, no longer concerned about his patch of grass or a blue ribbon.

Autopsy

By Mizeta Moon

It's my job to piece together what happened and clarify events that led to the corpse I was examining. The how, not why, of murder.

There was a faint breath of life left in this one when she was found. That tiny flame expired before her lips could utter names of her tormenters. All I knew about her was that she'd been the daughter of a wealthy businessman and was kidnapped by crankster-gangsters in broad daylight.

The reason I got this job is my high level of psychic awareness. Whenever I touch bruises or cuts, I receive mental pictures of how they occurred. It's like viewing a movie of what the victim saw and felt when the injury was inflicted. She had so many traumas on every part of her body that it was hard to know where to start. I knew what the circular abrasions around her ankles were before I touched them. When I did, my mind was assaulted by a leering, bearded face, so filled with menace that I temporarily recoiled. I was terrified, and my work had only just begun. Before continuing, I gulped some rancid office coffee in an attempt to steel my nerves.

I began to unravel a sequence of events. After being transported to a drug house, she'd been stripped naked in a room filled with skinheads. She could do nothing to prevent the sexual indignities that followed. Eventually, they suspended her by ropes and used her belly as a table where they laid out lines of crank and snorted them off of her. The chemicals burned her skin. She was nearly in a coma when taken to a cold shower and scrubbed head-to-toe with stiff brushes. She nearly drowned while they washed her hair. Her screams turned into whimpering sobs and free-flowing tears.

They dressed her in a flimsy cotton dress without bra or panties, then dragged her to a dirty old car. The license plate number became a repeating sequence in my mind. She had memorized it by saying it over and over in her head. I wrote it down for the cops to deal with when I filed my report. I took a few sips of the now cold coffee before resuming my gruesome task.

The menacing bearded face belonged to the leader of a bike gang she was sold to next. After receiving their payoff in meth, the kidnappers left her with these new monsters. The bikers used her, but didn't damage her badly, as they had plans. With legs in irons and naked once again, she huddled against a wet concrete wall in a tiny uncarpeted room without heat or light.

Someone finally brought her a stale donut and lukewarm milk. She could barely swallow, as her throat and mouth were sore and badly bruised. After what seemed like hours, a well-dressed man wearing a mask entered the room and examined her, while a floodlight played over private parts and dazzled her eyes. The man paid the bikers for her and had them wrap her in a dirty sheet, then tie it in a bundle before depositing her into the trunk of his car. The sheet had a tiny hole in it. She managed to look through it and memorize the license plate. Throughout her ordeal, she continuously thought of escape and reprisal.

The journey must have been quite lengthy, as I began to draw erratic images and felt tapped into other segments of her life. When the trunk finally opened, it was nearly as dark outside as it had been inside. Her new owner removed her bindings, then tethered and marched her into a poorly-lighted room where she could see people seated in randomly arranged chairs.

She was bound to a post rising from a dais in the center of the room. A spotlight focused on her nude figure, leaning tiredly against coarse wood. A fleshy man with a huge moustache acted as auctioneer while members of the audience bid for five-minute sessions with her. They could flog her, or perform heinous sex acts during their time.

The crowd paid to both watch and participate in blood-letting, so the whip came out more often than penetration occurred. Soon, she was a huddled mass of what used to be a human being. Soul broken. Mind gone. Body dying. They bundled her back into the sheet she arrived in, and without ceremony, placed her in the landfill. She was found by a couple of scavenging winos who told a beat cop about her in exchange for money to buy a gallon of wine. When the ambulance arrived, she was still breathing, but after three blocks, she died.

I've always hated the next part of my job. Not only do I have to type a full report for downtown, I have to relay my findings to the next of kin in person. As part of the legal process by which psychics took over the autopsy business, I am required to give full disclosure to the limits of their endurance, unless they sign a waiver. I put a blank waiver in my pocket, and slugged down bitter dregs of my coffee before tenderly covering her and exiting the autopsy room.

In my van, I fingered the waiver, hoping this was a story I would not have to tell. Knocking on the door of the parental home, I kept hoping, but those hopes were in vain. Her father invited me in, and after refusing to sign the waiver, bid me tell the whole story. It was when I got to the part of the well-dressed man buying her that I finally focused on her father's shoes.

When I did, memories came roaring into my mind. Fear clenched my throat and bile filled my mouth. Every fiber of my being screamed that I'd seen those shoes before. It was an effort to remain calm as I worked my way to the end, and got a signature on the form, stating I'd executed my duties. After leaving the house, I fumbled my phone from my pocket with shaking fingers. The principals of this tragedy were jailed within hours, but nothing could bring her back to life, or assuage her suffering.

Later, unwinding over a double martini, I thought about what a sick world we live in. What if the man had been in his slippers? Had he simply signed the waiver, is it possible the truth would never come out? The why of his actions and depth of his depravity were not my department. Tomorrow would bring yet another corpse, so there was little time to ponder more than the next few moments, and whether I would have another drink.

When Too Much Is Enough
By Howard Schneider

"Go away!" Garth screamed out of a dream, lashing out with his leg, nearly kicking his partner, Harley, off his side of the bed. At only a hundred-thirty pounds, Harley was dwarfed by Garth's two-eighty, easily overcome by the sheer power of his bulk.

"Quit that!" Harley said, smacking the sweat-drenched, yellowed sheet twisted around the lower portion of Garth's huge body.

Garth rolled off his back toward the opposite wall, expelled a loud fart and resumed the snorting that had kept Harley awake most of the night.

Harley glanced at the alarm clock on the shelf, barely visible in the dim light spilling through a torn and lop-sided moldy shade partially obscuring the tiny bedroom's only window. It was six-ten.

May as well get up. No chance of sleep now.

In the cramped kitchen, Harley added a heaping teaspoon of fresh coffee to leftover grounds and pressed the ON button. He then retrieved the *Yuma Star* from outside the door. He relished this precious early-morning time to himself. The eight-dollars-a-month subscription was the only luxury he permitted himself, or, for that matter, could afford.

Around nine, only halfway through the sports section, he heard the toilet flush, then a door slam shut. He looked up as Garth stumbled along a short, narrow hallway that connected the bedroom to the kitchen area, his grubby hands pressing against plastic-veneer walls as he edged forward. Without a word to Harley, he went directly to the under-counter fridge and retrieved a 32 ounce half-empty bottle of Coca-Cola, then took a dirty glass out of a little sink and filled it.

He squeezed onto the bench-seat across from Harley, took a long pull on the Coke, then said, "You gonna get that air conditioner fixed this morning? It's gonna reach 124 today."

"I told you yesterday, we gotta wait till social security comes. We're down to nothing. Ain't no way to pay the $85 it's gonna cost," Harley said, reaching for the coffee pot.

"What am I supposed to do? Roast in this hell-hot oven of a shit hole?"

"Well, you could go to the senior center over on Campbell Street. They got a cooling center. Least that's what they call it."

"I ain't gonna sit around doing nothing with a bunch of brain-dead old geezers, staring at the walls and waiting for some do-good-er volunteer to mop up their drool."

"Suit yourself, Garth. But I'm gonna go out to the shed before it gets too hot and make more coasters for the gift shop at the bus station. They sold the last of 'em yesterday and want more. They owe me $26. That'll keep us in beer and lunch meat for a few days. Pay for some gas, too. You need more cigarettes?"

"Listen here, you skinny little shitdog. You know damn-well I do. I told you that last night. And you know you gotta get the air conditioner fixed, no matter how you do it. So get your ass in gear. When my daddy died, he left this trailer to me, not you. If you wanna keep living here, you better damn-well do what I say. I'm tired of you taking advantage of me. You being my live-in don't mean nothing when it comes to who's running the show around this place. I ain't as stupid as you think. I know what you're trying to do. Steal everything I got? That's your plan, ain't it?"

Harley didn't say a word. He drained the last of his coffee, carefully folded the paper and laid it on the seat next to him, then looked at Garth. He wanted to look away, away from the snot oozing from his nose, from his bloodshot eyes. But he didn't.

"Garth. First, you're wrong about that. Second. You got to accept that we don't got the money to fix the damn air conditioner. The appliance shop turned me down when I tried to buy a new one on credit. Said I weren't credit-worthy. I told you, I'll take care of it next week when my check comes. So shut up about it and do the best you can."

Garth slapped his fat fist onto the table, rattling Harley's cup and bouncing his glass. He spilled Coke down his chin and onto the sour-smelling Daffy Duck tee shirt he slept in, as he gulped another big swallow, then yelled, "You little rat turd. Who do you think you are, telling me to shut up. Get the hell outta my trailer. And get that crap of yours outta the shed. The few lousy dollars you bring in from that junk you make out of that scrap wood ain't worth the mess and noise you make. And don't come back unless you got a working air conditioner." Struggling, he got up from the narrow bench seat and headed towards an old TV that sat on a rickety wooden crate in front of a threadbare, faded lime-green, two-cushion sofa.

Harley slid off his seat, carefully placed his cup in amongst the dirty dishes in the sink, then went to the door to the outside where he stood for a moment looking through its little window. He didn't bother to answer Garth's threat, didn't even look at him. He went out and closed the door behind him. He threaded his way through junk scattered around a little packed-dirt yard, and made his way around a stack of old bald tires to the shed where he had his workbench and tools. He unlocked it and went straight to a pile of scavenged wood. He selected a length of mesquite branch, secured it in the bench vise, took down a saw from where it hung on a pegboard on the wall above the bench, and got to work. He tried to forget about Garth and his threats, but no matter how hard he tried, couldn't get him out of his mind.

When Harley returned to the trailer several hours later, Garth was standing in front of the TV messing with the rabbit ears, swearing a blue streak at the flickering image on the screen. His broad back was to him, having not turned around when Harley came in.

"You got that air conditioner? If you don't, you can get the hell outta here," Garth said, intent on adjusting the picture.

Harley moved behind Garth, waited a moment until the big man was perfectly still, then with a powerful arching swing, smashed the claw side of a 22-ounce framing hammer into the top of Garth's sweaty bald head. He heard it crack through bone and felt it continue all the way down as far as it could go. Garth was already dead when he crashed across the TV and then down to the ratty carpet. His blood soaked into the dirty shag as fast as it spurted from the gaping hole left behind when Harley pulled the hammer away. As he did, he said, "No, Garth. I don't have the air conditioner."

He wiped the bloody hammer clean on Daffy Duck, then went back out to the shed and rehung it in its rightful place.

Harley was standing on the step about to open the trailer door when he noticed a woman walking towards him. An ancient gray-muzzled cocker spaniel wobbled behind her on a long leash, nosing along the edge of the asphalt as she pulled and jerked it forward.

"Morning, Harley. I come to visit Garth. Maybe watch one of our programs. We like the same ones, you know."

"Hey, Sally. How you doing? Garth don't feel so good this morning. He's got a bad headache. Came on real sudden-like."

"Well, I'll check on him. See if there's anything he needs," Sally said, jerking the dog away from a broken bird bath lying on its side. You want to hold on to Perky, or should I tie her to the post?" she said, indicating the mailbox nearby.

"No. That won't do. He went back to bed and is sound asleep. Anyway, we're leaving when he wakes up. Going up to Kingman to visit his cousin. He'll be back in a few weeks."

"Kinda sudden, ain't it? He never said nothing about that yesterday. He never said anything about a cousin, either."

"Yeah, I know. They weren't close. Been years since he's heard from him. He called this morning. Gonna have some kinda operation. Wanted to see Garth again. Maybe he's worried or something. Who knows? Anyway, we're leaving soon as he wakes up," he told her again.

"Well, stop by on your way out if you want. I'd like to say goodbye," Sally said, turning back the way she came and tugging on the leash.

"We'll do that," Harley called after her.

When Sally was out of sight, Harley went back into the trailer. Five minutes later he came out carrying a little duffle bag and a cardboard box tied with string and tossed them into his beat-up Ford Ranger pickup. He then went to the shed and threw some tools into a rusty toolbox, took it out to the truck and secured it in the bed.

Smiling, he climbed into the cab, turned up the volume on a country station and drove off, thinking about which direction to take after he collected his $26, and then made it out to the Interstate.

Recall

By Mizeta Moon

"Hello," the electronic voice said in mellifluous tones meant to pave the way for what could only be bad news. I'd heard this greeting several times in the past few years when something I purchased failed or was facing recall. What was it now? I wondered. Steeling myself, I resisted the urge to hang up and let the message go to voice mail.

When I didn't disconnect, the voice continued.

"I am sorry to inform you that materials from your recent penis enhancement have been deemed hazardous to long-term health of other organs you've upgraded. A manufacturer's recall has resulted in your eligibility for a new penis, using an exciting state-of-the-art material that is both highly sensitive and durable under extreme performance conditions."

I was dismayed. I'd only had the new one for two years and it was working fine. Why now, when I'd just met a hottie at the Sunset Home for Swinging Seniors? After all, it was the year 2135 and everyone was constantly adding new parts in order to live longer. Shouldn't manufacturers have it figured out by now?

"If you would like to make an appointment with a local transplant clinic, please press the star key now. If you choose to continue using your present device, be advised that your health insurance carrier may terminate coverage for your liver, lung, and eye transplants our records show are still under warranty."

What could I do but comply? Pressing the star key, I waited patiently while another electronic voice detailed my options. Choosing number nine, I was told that all available appointments for penile exchange were booked for the next three months. Sighing, I accepted a date that would interfere with the annual toga party at Sheba's Sensual Spa, which had always been a highlight of the social season for me. I guessed there would always be next year, as long as my heart, whose warranty had expired, was still healthy enough for sex.

Busking

By Howard Schneider

It was impossible to overlook the stooped and fragile-looking old man standing under the overhang of the Hollywood Rite Aid Pharmacy. He had on at least three over-sized raggedy sweaters, filthy corduroys and beat up, worn down high-top tennis shoes. An empty shoe box sat on the sidewalk in front of him. At least he was dry, although the endless Portland winter drizzle must have given him a chill, as it most likely did to the steady stream of people passing by.

When he began singing, even though at first softly, a few of those walking past stopped to listen. Maybe it was curiosity, or perhaps the old gospel hymn that anyone remotely acquainted with music would recognize. But even if it weren't familiar to some, his far-from-perfect rendition was impossible to ignore.

> **Amazing grace how sweet the sound**
> **That saved a wretch like me.**
> **I once was lost but now I'm found**
> **Was blind but now I see**

Suddenly he stopped singing and said, "I'm sorry, folks, I can't do this . . .

Silent and unmoving, he stared off into the distance for a few seconds. After a few seconds, he nodded his head, as if in response to some unseen vision, or a secret message intended only for him, and then said, "Okay, Mama. I'll be good. Like you told me to."

Then he began singing again. Only this time it was . . .

Just a closer walk with Thee

**Grant it, Jesus, is my plea
Daily walking close to Thee**

But then he stopped again, this time looking up into the heavens and crying out in desperation, "Mama! I can't do this no more. Please don't make me. You know I love you, but I just can't." Pleading bordering on panic was palpable in his every word.

He then lowered his gaze to the group gathered around him, which by then had grown to twenty or more people. As he looked into the eyes of all those staring back at him, they must have felt that he sensed their empathy, or perhaps sensed their concern. Because with the twitch of a fleeting smile, he stood erect, held his head higher, tapped his foot a few times and broke into song . . .

**When you are sad and lonely, and have no place to go
Come and see me baby, and bring along some dough
And we'll go honky tonkin', honky tonkin'
Honky tonkin', honey baby,
We'll go honky tonkin' 'round this town**

Then, like before, he stopped. But this time he turned to the wall and crashed his forehead against the cold concrete and started crying. His shoulders heaved in time to his anguished sobs, and he beat his fists against the hard surface as if pounding out a rhythm of deep despair.

The onlookers, by then numbering 30 or so, expanding off the sidewalk into the rain-swollen gutter, seemed confused or embarrassed, and whispered among themselves. But they remained where they stood, as if waiting for some kind of explanation, as if needing to understand what this poor tormented man was suffering.

Then one of them, a young woman smartly dressed in tweed and wearing sensible brown leather pumps, stepped forward and went to stand at his side. She placed her arm around his shoulders and said a few words, too softly for the crowd to hear. The old man stopped crying and beating at the wall and looked at her. She spoke a few more words. He nodded and said something to her. She then took her arm away from his shoulders and returned to where she had been standing before.

The old man turned back to the circle of onlookers. His body shifted as if a heavy weight had been lifted off his back. He slowly surveyed their questioning faces, then began to sing again.

> **I come to the garden alone,**
> **While the dew is still on the roses**
> **And the voice I hear,**
> **Falling on my ear...**

But he stopped abruptly and lifted his eyes to heaven and screamed, "Sorry, Lord. I can't do it. I gotta sing what *I* want to. Not what Mama always wanted."

Then, without hesitation, he started again,

> **When you and your baby have a fallin' out,**
> **Just call me up sweet mama and we'll go steppin' out.**
> **And we'll go honky tonkin', honky tonkin'.**
> **Honky tonkin', honey baby,**
> **We'll go honky tonkin' 'round this town**

The vitality and passion he projected in a half dozen more Hank Williams numbers infected his audience with the same energy. As he plunged ahead, singing what he wanted to, it was obvious to all in the crowd, which was by then captivated by the old man's performance, that his heart was in those songs—and they loved it. Off-pitch, wrong words, erratic rhythm and all, they ate it up. It was like feeding candy to little kids.

When he ended with "I'm So Lonesome I Could Cry," and thanked the people for being there, the appreciative listeners told him how much they liked his singing and urged him not to worry about trying to please his mother, and that he should follow his own instincts. That he should sing what he wanted to and not be restricted by the dictates of anyone else, especially dead relatives. And, as if propelled by forces beyond their comprehension, they filled his box to overflowing with coins and bills, and even a few checks.

After the crowd dispersed, and he had retrieved the box full of money, a big late-model Mercedes sedan snaked up to the curb where he patiently stood waiting.

"Get in out of the rain, Papa! You'll catch your death of cold," the young woman in the tweed business suit sitting behind the wheel said when he opened the door. "How'd we do? Looks like a good haul."

"Yeah. It is. With what we did downtown this morning, we should be close to six or seven hundred."

"Well, you did real good. Although maybe you went a little heavy on the drama about your *mama* wanting you to sing that religious stuff."

"Hey. It worked, didn't it? But I'm sure as hell getting tired of that Hank Williams crap. Think I'm gonna do go back to my Elvis routine tomorrow. I'll hit 'em with "Blue Suede Shoes," and end with "Jailhouse Rock." That one always brings in the money."

Wheelchair Power
By Howard Schneider

Chapter One

Portland, Oregon; Wednesday, 7:20 a.m.

I surveyed the rise ahead. Not with worry or apprehension, but anticipation, perhaps how an Olympian runner might feel waiting for the crack of the starter's pistol. My destination was the bus stop just beyond the crest of the hill, a mere three blocks away. Over the past eleven years, after overcoming depression at being sentenced to a manual wheelchair . . . non-motorized by choice, I came to accept, even cherish, the exertion of daily workouts, efforts that years before had transformed what once had been a weakling's body into a well-muscled powerhouse. Approaching the incline with confidence was further proof of my dominance over the post-polio syndrome that shrank my legs to little more than lifeless sticks. During rare bouts of self-pity, I reminisced about how in my twenties I ran 5-K races. Never winning, but always elated just to reach the finish line. Recovery from childhood polio was a great blessing; its return two decades later was an unwelcome cruelty. But with time, I grew to forgo self-pity and accept the reality of my current life. To relish the elation of racing along a sidewalk or street under my own propulsion, wind in my face and pleasant fatigue in my muscles. Even more important is the fact that self-pity does nothing to help me pursue the objectives of my life, including my job hawking the daily newspaper along a stretch of Portland's Southeast Hawthorne Boulevard known as "Alcohol Alley," and where I was now headed.

I love my newspaper job: the friends, the conversations, the warm reception in the pubs and bars that dominate these blocks.

This is an important part of my life. True, there may be an occasional expression of pity from some for a poor cripple peddling newspapers, but I don't let that bother me. I've learned that a little pity can be good for business, as it's usually accompanied by big tips. No! . . . I don't object to a little pity, especially in the form of a smile and a well-intentioned five- or ten-dollar bill and, more importantly, by absolute trust in me as a non-threatening friend and confidant. But this outward aspect of who I am, who the world sees, is a mere charade. It's not all that I am. This charade, however, serves a purpose, and that is what this story is about.

When the bus came to a complete stop, I wheeled into the aisle and waited for the chair ramp to complete its downward sweep.

"Clank!" It landed on the sidewalk with an abrupt halt.

"Good to go," Barney the driver said.

"Thanks, man. See you later. I'll be finished around noon," I replied on my way down the ramp.

"See you then, buddy. I'll still be on this route," he yelled, watching me roll out onto Hawthorne.

Half a block east, two bundles of newspapers were waiting exactly where they should be, on a worn wooden bench chained to a wall next to the front door of Chubb's Cafe. Twisting halfway round, I tossed the bundles into my rear cargo basket, then wheeled through the entry door and headed to my usual table in the back corner, a spot where my chair wouldn't be in anybody's way.

"Morning, Chubb. What's new?" I said as I passed a middle-aged woman behind the counter filling a mug with fresh coffee.

"You seem chipper this morning. What's up with you?"

"Nose to the grindstone like any other day." I greeted a few of the other regular customers as I made my way past them, and nodded to an elderly man I had not seen before. He was sitting with a smartly dressed middle-age woman who looked vaguely familiar, but at the moment I couldn't place. Maybe because I was looking forward to the first swig of coffee that Chubb was delivering to my table and which I was much in need of.

"Two pancakes, one egg over easy, crispy bacon, and whole-wheat toast," I said when Chubb stood waiting for my order.

"You ever gonna try something different? You've been having the same goddamn breakfast since you've been coming here. How about biscuits and gravy? Or a Belgian waffle? Or liver and onions?"

"Two pancakes, one egg over easy, crispy bacon, and whole-wheat toast," I repeated, giving her my best smile.

"Right. Enjoy your coffee," she replied, grinning over her shoulder as she marched off to the kitchen to prepare what I assume she already knew I was going to order.

After the first taste of what was undeniably the best cup of coffee in Portland, I retrieved the bundles of papers, sat them on the chair next to me, took out my pocketknife and cut the twine that held them together, then made a quick count. I'm a stickler for procedure, and always make sure that I get what I'm being charged for. Only once was the count off. That time there were two papers too many; 52 instead of 50. By reporting that discrepancy to my delivery guy, and paying for them (I had been able to sell the extras), I established my credibility and set a standard for honesty that has served me well over the seven years that I've been doing this.

As if Chubb were on an immutable schedule, as soon as I had the papers arranged in pouches on the sides of my chair, from which they were easily accessed for delivery or hawking, she set my breakfast in front of me. It was steaming hot and accompanied by a fresh refill of her special-brewed Stumptown breakfast blend, fat-free milk on the side.

I savored her gourmet offering with gusto rather than haste. I ate slowly, with deeply-felt appreciation, relishing not only the perfection of freshness and flavors, but also the care with which she prepared my simple meal. Chubb knew what it meant to me; how this time in her safe haven allowed me to prepare for a morning of hustling, dealing with the usual challenges to the disabled, and, occasionally, with jerks that sometimes complicate my life. But there were some things she had no idea about, the existence of my other life, and how it might unfold in the hours ahead.

After I mopped up the last of the egg with the toast and signaled for a refill, the two newcomers, the elderly man and woman with him that I had noticed upon my arrival, approached my table. Now my real work began.

Chapter Two

Portland, Oregon; Wednesday, 12:35 p.m.

Barney knew my stop and gently merged to the curb as I approached the front exit. Down the ramp onto the sidewalk, I headed north three blocks, then west six. At my gate, recessed into an eight-foot-high English laurel hedge that spanned half the block, I entered the password after making sure no one was watching and wheeled through after it swung open. Behind me its soft closure, punctuated with a quiet click, ushered me into the seclusion of my private world. Arvin stood at the front door with a welcoming smile.

"How was your morning, sir?" he said as I propelled my chair into a wide entry hall.

"Good! Progress on all fronts. There *is* a new wrinkle we need to sort out, though. But first, lunch. Any idea what Ginger might surprise us with today?"

"From fragrances drifting from her kitchen, I would guess Southeast Asian. Shall I open a Chablis? I brought up and cooled a '93, just in case."

After washing up, I joined Arvin in the formal dining room which also served as a conference room. Ginger, like Arvin, had been employed by my parents for years. After Mom and Dad were caught fourteen years ago by a sneaker wave in the Oregon coast town of Manzanita, I was fortunate that these loyal servants agreed to remain with me. Arvin, and his partner Phillip, who also happened to be my personal attendant, have rooms above the three-car garage, and Ginger has a suite on the second floor. Even though there is an elevator from the basement to the ground floor and on to the upstairs level, I keep to the ground floor; a gym and a large bedroom and bath suite more than meet all my needs.

As was our custom, Arvin and I waited until dessert and coffee to get to work, reserving the meal for talk of local politics, and reviewing my investments. After my parents' death, I divested the sprawling business empire my father had created, and Arvin does an excellent job of keeping the resulting fortune working in my favor.

After the table was cleared, Ginger brought in a fresh pot of coffee and placed it on the hotplate.

"Thank you for that delicious curry," I said as she started to leave.

"My mother's recipe. The secret is to sauté the shrimp before adding to the sauce. With mustard oil only. Also you must grind mustard seed just before using; that's the Kerala way to make the best flavor."

With that treasured morsel of culinary perfection conveyed, she returned to the sanctity of her kitchen, once again satisfied with the outcome of her effort to match her mother's skills.

Arvin refilled our cups, then fired up his laptop.

"What is the wrinkle you mentioned before lunch, sir?"

"Jack Hackett. He was paroled from prison yesterday, sooner than anticipated. Jack's ex-girlfriend, Carrie, and her uncle, an ex-con named Dick Gaines, visited me at Chubb's this morning. She's scared Hackett will find her. He threatened to kill her after she testified against him at his trial. Last night she got a call from his cousin Vince. He told her that Jack is asking around about where she lives or works."

"Hackett's a nasty piece of work," agreed Arvin. "Shall I have Rantman see if he can get a line on Hackett's whereabouts? If I remember correctly, Rantman knew some of his old pals and hangouts."

"Yes. If anyone can locate Hackett, Rantman can. He's the best finder around. But nothing more than just finding him. No rough stuff. I'll take care of that myself. It's personal. After the trial he threatened to kill me, too. Because I helped Carrie. If there's one thing I don't like, it's being threatened, especially by a lowlife like Hackett. Let me know as soon as Rantman contacts you, if he does, that is."

Arvin tapped out a few lines, then hit "send."

"What's next on your list, sir?"

After dispensing with a half-dozen outstanding items, and assessing a couple of new requests I got while peddling papers that morning, it was time for the gym. I work hard to maintain my strength in preparation for the leg prostheses that I had commissioned and were now in development. I wasn't going to let weakness in my legs prevent me from having as strong an upper body as possible. I am determined to be in top form for when I'm whole again.

"Any progress on the robot legs?" I asked Arvin as I wheeled along the hall to the gym.

"Yes, sir. Dr. Talbert called this morning. They expect the new prototype to be ready by the end of the week. Apparently, an algorithm that controlled something for the last legs you tested was defective. He said the nerve interface didn't work right; inappropriate micro-compatibility or some such thing. He thinks we'll have it Friday. He seemed sort of optimistic."

"Good. I hope this time they get it right. I'm beginning to wonder, though. It's been almost a year and still no success."

"Yes. That's true, but it does appear to be a rather difficult challenge. Is there anything else, sir?"

"Yes. Get Betty on the phone for me. And make sure there's a bottle of Dom Perignon on ice for this evening."

"Certainly, sir. If that's everything then, after I connect you with Betty I'll get on with our work."

"Thank you, Arvin. I'll be in the gym for the next hour. Please let Zachary know."

Arvin started to walk away, but suddenly stopped and took his iPhone from his blazer pocket. He looked at it for a moment, then said, "A text from Rantman. He located Hackett. He's holed up in an RV park in Estacada with a guy he knew in prison."

Rantman found Hackett sooner than I had anticipated. But I shouldn't have been surprised; Rantman's good at what he does. That's why I use him, and pay him well. I trust him to keep quiet about whatever's between us: no leaks, no loose talk. As far as the world is concerned, we don't even know each other. Which is essentially true since we've never met in person. Why should we? We're business associates, not friends.

"Forget about calling Betty," I said as Arvin headed along the hall toward his office. "Call Calvin. See if he's available tonight. I'm all of a sudden in the mood for a visit to Estacada."

"Are you sure, sir? It could be dangerous," Arvin said after he turned to face me. "Hackett is an evil monster." Unconcealed concern spread across his face.

"Arvin. Please, just call him. I'll be okay."

"I know you will. I'll do it now," he mumbled as he turned to leave.

After Arvin dug around on the internet and made a few phone calls, he joined me a half-hour later in the gym. "Hackett's prison buddy is Buster Landis. He was released six months ago after an eight-year stretch for assault and battery, attempted burglary and possession of a lethal weapon. Seems he was captured in the act by the victim's protection dog; twenty-two stitches in his right arm. Rumor has it that he's easing back into dealing guns, drugs and stolen cars. Certainly not one of our upstanding citizens."

"Right," I yelled at Arvin over the clanking noise as he started back to his office and as I increased the weight on the bicep curl machine.

I wasn't surprised by Hackett's choice of friends, or that after twelve years in the pen he was still determined to take revenge on Carrie. That's the kind of guy he is, a violent psychopath. Back then, he made the mistake of bragging to Carrie about robbing a 7-Eleven, even showed her the gun and the sack of money. A whole box of Butterfingers, too. Hackett was arrested in short order thanks to the store's security camera and his mug shots on file as part of a long criminal record. Carrie, an ex-meth addict suddenly with nowhere to live, found herself in need of a lawyer to deal with the DA's trumped-up charge about her being an accomplice to Hackett's crime. I learned about her situation from her cousin, Boyko Petkov, a bartender at one of the Hawthorne bars where I sell papers. Boyko had done me some favors, so I told him I'd help Carrie. I set her up in an apartment, then hooked her up with Monica Silber, one of the trial lawyers at the law firm I use. The price for my help was her keeping on the straight and narrow: no drugs and no hanging out with bad characters.

At the trial, Carrie had told all, realizing it was her ticket to escape Hackett and his unbridled brutality. The DA got Hackett convicted and Monica got the DA off of Carrie's back. Monica also managed to obtain a permanent injunction against Hackett ever seeing Carrie again. When I saw Boyko a few months after the trial, he said Carrie had a job in a bar in Vancouver, was making a decent living, had a boyfriend, and was staying clean. After twelve years, Carrie had a new look: a different hair style and color, and wearing glasses. I didn't recognize her when I first saw her at Chubb's this morning. But it appears that she's held up her end of our bargain, so I'll hold up mine. I'd invested a lot in this woman and wasn't going to allow a deranged criminal like Hackett to do her harm.

As Zachary was helping me out of the Jacuzzi, Arvin came into the gym and said, "Calvin will be here around eight."

"Good," I replied. "Would you please make sure the van has a full tank of gas?"

Chapter Three

Portland, Oregon; Wednesday, 7:57 p.m.

Arvin buzzed the gate for Calvin and told him to meet me in the garage. We were on the road in my modified Dodge van five minutes later. I drove, Calvin rode shotgun.

"What's the agenda? Arvin didn't say when he called," Calvin asked as we merged onto the highway and headed east.

Calvin, an ex-Marine and fifteen years my senior, had done special assignments for my dad's law firm, and was always willing to back me up when it came to touchy situations like tonight's. He was as close to family as I had, and I knew I could count on him if things got out of hand.

"We need to find Jack Hackett and convince him to stay away from his old girlfriend, Carrie. According to Rantman, word on the street is that he intends to get even for her testifying against him at his trial. He got ten years in prison based on her testimony, and he's not the kind that forgives and forgets."

"I didn't know the bastard was out. Why Estacada?" Calvin asked.

"He's only been out a few days, but Rantman tracked him down in an RV park out there. He's bunking with another ex-con, Buster Landis, a low-life drug dealer who traffics in guns and stolen cars. There could be fireworks. Are you prepared?'

"Aren't I always?" Calvin said, then pulled a Glock semiautomatic pistol from a holster under his left arm and checked the rounds.

"I don't want any gunplay, just want to give him a friendly warning. But be ready for anything, you never know what'll happen."

"I was born ready," Calvin replied, jamming the pistol back

into its holster.

Forty-three minutes later I pulled into an empty slot in the park, cut the lights and engine, and checked my GPS.

"Buster's space should be at the end of this row. Must be that one," I said, pointing through the front window. "I'll wheel up there in my chair, knock on the door and have a friendly talk with Hackett. Let him know that his parole officer wouldn't be exactly thrilled that he's keeping company with a known felon. That I wouldn't hesitate one minute to give the officer a heads-up if I learn that he gets anywhere near Carrie."

"And if he's not there?" Calvin asked, fully aware that my plan was iffy, to say the least.

"I'll try to squeeze out where he is from whoever is there."

"How do you plan to do that?"

"Money talks, right?"

"Sometimes. What do you want me to do in case it doesn't tonight?"

"Follow close, but stay out of sight. I don't want Hackett, or anybody else, to think there's a threat of danger."

I banged on the door of an ancient, rundown, rust-covered RV. It cracked open barely enough for a scrawny woman with scraggly hair and rotten teeth to peek out. She looked scared, and she shifted back and forth from one foot to the other.

"What you want? Who are you?"

"A friend of Jack Hackett's. Is he here?"

"No. He ain't."

"How about Buster?"

"What do you want with him?" she asked, worry revealed in her raspy voice. She glanced to her side, then quickly stepped away.

Suddenly the door flew open, missing my face by less than an inch as it whizzed past. "Who the hell are you?" a shirtless tall and lanky man demanded as he appeared in the open doorway. He held his right hand behind his back, as if concealing something.

He looked down at me and said, "You must be that son-of-a-bitch do-gooder that screwed my buddy ten years ago. You got that shyster lawyer for his double-crossing girlfriend. It's a good thing he's not here or you'd be dead meat. What do you want?"

"He and I need to talk. Where can I find him?" I said, ignoring his bravado.

"Get the hell outta here before I kick your ass halfway to hell, you useless cripple."

"I've got something for him," I lied, again ignoring his threat. "A cash settlement for the pain I caused him. I feel bad that I was partially responsible for his incarceration."

The anger creasing his goateed face quickly changed to a look of confusion. "Are you shitting me? You got it with you?"

Having anticipated how this strategy might play out, I withdrew a bulging envelope from my tote bag and waved it at him. "Ten large to help ease his way back into society."

"Jack's not here. Leave it with me. I'll give it to him," Buster said, stepping down onto a narrow moss-covered wood platform in front of the door. He stuck out his left hand, keeping his right one out of sight.

"I'd rather give it to him myself," I said, rolling the chair back a few feet.

"I said I'd give it to him. Hand it over!" He then swung his right arm around and stuck a pistol in my face.

I glanced at a barely detectable movement in the shadows at the edge of the RV, then instantly returned my gaze to Buster. "If I were you, I'd drop that weapon."

Before Buster could reply, Calvin appeared as if out of nowhere and pressed the barrel of his Glock against the side of Buster's tattooed bald head. "The man said drop the gun. Do it or lose your brains. I realize it may not be much of a loss, but I do think you'd miss them."

Buster dropped the weapon and Calvin kicked it away. Then, without warning, he slammed Buster with a powerful punch to his gut. Buster doubled over in pain, but managed to remain on his feet.

"Now, Buster," I said after he regained his breath, "how about telling us where your buddy Hackett is. I'm not going to do him harm, or cause trouble with his parole officer. Where did he go?"

"Fuck you, asshole," Buster answered through clenched teeth.

Before I could repeat my question, Calvin pointed his silenced Glock at Buster's foot and fired a single round.

Buster screamed and fell onto the dead grass that passed for the RV's front yard. Blood oozed from a gaping hole in his snake-skin cowboy boot. When he started to get back up from where he had collapsed, Calvin stomped hard on his bleeding foot, then pushed him back down.

Buster screamed, but nobody came to his rescue. The trailer door remained shut. His woman stayed inside, well out of the line of fire.

"Let's try again," I said, looking down at the man sprawled on the ground in front of me, whimpering like a hurt dog. "Tell us where Hackett is. Or does my friend have to resort to more aggressive methods to persuade you of our determination to find him?"

Calvin only needed the threat of a shot to the other foot to convince Buster to talk. "He left about half an hour ago in my truck to find some guy named Dick Gaines. His old girlfriend's uncle. He found out from his cousin Vinnie that Gains hangs out most nights at a bar in North Portland called Toby's Millhouse." Buster also said that Hackett was high on meth and had taken one of his pistols.

I had met Gaines when he and Carrie sought my help at Chubb's that morning, and I knew he'd be no match for Hackett, especially if Hackett was jacked up on drugs. We had to get to Gaines before Hackett did. If not, he might tell Hackett where Carrie lived.

Calvin quickly searched the RV and found two mobile phones, which he crushed under his heel. He then warned Buster not to try and contact Hackett if he valued his miserable life. As an extra measure, he cuffed Buster and the woman, hands and feet, and left them in the tiny bedroom with its door jammed shut.

"You better call Carrie and tell her to get to a safe place, just in case we don't get to Gaines in time enough," Calvin said as we got into the van.

"I don't know her number. And I don't know where she lives, either. I'll put Arvin on it. He can call Carrie's cousin Boyko at the pub on Hawthorne where he tends bar," I replied, punching in Arvin's code on the van's auto dialer.

While I drove, Calvin Googled Toby's bar. It was on Interstate Avenue near Lombard.

"We'll be there in about 30 minutes," I said. "Hold on, this is going to be a fast ride."

Back on the interstate and encountering little traffic, I said, "You got pretty rough with Buster. Was all that necessary? I was hoping to do this without resorting to violence."

"Violence is what guys like Buster understand. And we're in a hurry, aren't we? You can't have it both ways, boss."

I didn't respond. He was right; sometimes it's a balance between expediency and the means to achieve it. With Buster, the balance point had not been in his favor. I didn't like the way it went, but under the circumstances, had no grounds for objection.

We pulled into a parking spot behind Toby's 27 minutes later. It was a shabby, windowless, one-story cinderblock building badly in need of paint. The rear lot was half full, six cars, but no truck that matched Buster's.

Inside, we encountered a dimly-lit smoke-filled room smelling of beer and unwashed old men; Hank Williams' plaintive I'm So Lonesome I Could Cry crackled over scratchy ceiling speakers. A dozen or so patrons, some at the bar, most in booths, sat in stony silence. Gaines wasn't among them. The barman glanced at us, then turned his back and returned to the basketball game on a wall-mounted TV behind the bar.

"What'll you have?" the bartender asked when he turned around after Calvin slapped his hand down on the bar top.

"Some information. Has Dick Gaines been here tonight?"

"No idea who you're talking about. This ain't no information booth. You want something to drink?"

"No. I just want an answer to my question."

"If you ain't drinking, then you and your wheelchair buddy can get the hell out of here."

Calvin walked behind the bar to where the bartender stood, took a half-full bottle of Jamison off the liquor rack and smashed it into the TV screen, shattering it and the bottle. Glass shards and brown liquid rained down around them.

"The next one will be over your head," Calvin said to the shocked bartender.

"Are you crazy? I'm calling the cops," the bartender said, and picked up a cell phone off the back counter.

Calvin grabbed the phone out of his hand, smashed it down onto the bar, then dropped what was left of it into a bar sink filled with dirty soapy water. He took another bottle off the display shelf and holding it by its neck smashed it on the edge of the bar. He held the jagged edge of what was left an inch in front of the petrified barman's face.

"Let's start this conversation over. Dick Gaines? We know he hangs out here. What about tonight?"

The barman looked around the room, but nobody moved. No one said a word. He was on his own.

Calvin pushed the bottle shard closer, pricking the man's cheek so that blood ran down to his chin and dripped onto his shirt.

"He was here, but a guy came and took him away. The guy was wild, like he was drugged out, or just nuts. He threatened that if anybody said he was here he'd come back and kill all of us," the bartender finally blurted out.

"Did he say where he was taking Gaines?"

"No. He pulled Gaines outta that booth over there and walked him out the door, warning us as he left."

I wheeled closer to where Calvin stood, pulled a wad of money from my pocket, peeled off five one-hundred-dollar bills and threw them on the bar. "Sorry for the mess, but we're in a hurry."

"Let's go," I said as I spun round and headed for the door.

The first thing I did after we were back in the van was call Arvin. "Did you contact Carrie?"

"Couldn't find a number or address for her. I reached Boyko though, but he said he didn't know anything about her whereabouts. Said he'd lost touch with her a long time ago. Rantman's still searching, but it doesn't look good."

I doubted that Boyko was telling Arvin the truth; he and Carrie seemed to be close back when the trial was underway.

Arvin gave us Boyko's number and Calvin called on the speaker mode as I pulled out of the lot and headed to Hawthorne and the bar where Boyko worked. There was no answer, but Calvin got through on the bar's land line.

"Happy Days," a male voice answered.

"Can I speak with Boyko?" I said.

"Not now. Who's this?"

"A friend. It's urgent. I need to talk to him."

"Yeah. Well, maybe you can get hold of him at the hospital. Providence, on Northeast Glisan."

"What happened?"

"Some crazy asshole stormed in here, dragged him into the kitchen and beat him half to death. The guy left before the cops got here. He was nuts. Threatened the rest of us, but he only went after Boyko."

The emergency room was crowded with desperate patients, but with persuasive sincerity I convinced the besieged desk nurse to let us into the treatment area to see our "cousin" Boyko Petkov.

We found him in a curtained cubicle, the nurse having just given him something to ease his pain. He looked like he'd been run over by a Mack truck, but was awake and somewhat coherent.

"What did you tell him?" I asked, not bothering about details of his encounter with Hackett and the beating he had received. "Where's Carrie?" It took a couple of tries, but he finally replied, admitting he knew more than he told Arvin earlier.

"I couldn't help it. I told him where she lived in Vancouver. He was gonna burn out my eyes with a lit cigar. The guy's nuts. I managed to call Carrie after he left. She didn't answer, but I left messages about him coming for her. I hope she got it. Then I woke up in an ambulance, and now I'm here."

Back in the van, Calvin Googled Carrie's address while I headed up I-5 North to Vancouver. We arrived at an ostentatiously upscale condo twenty minutes later and pulled into a space behind a three-story unit, the southernmost end of a large triplex.

"This is pretty damn plush," Calvin observed.

"Yes, it is," I agreed, somewhat surprised at what we had discovered: classy brick and cedar siding, two big decks on each unit, lush landscaping and a swimming pool down the way.

"How does a bar waitress afford this?" Calvin asked.

I wondered the same, but didn't bother to answer. Instead, I pointed to a truck a few spaces away. "That pickup. Doesn't it match Buster's description of his?"

"Yeah, sure does. The bastard beat us here. The lights are on in her unit. Let's go!" Calvin said as he jumped out and ran around to where the chair lift would deposit me.

"How do you want to handle this?" Calvin asked as we hurried along a tree-lined walkway that led to the front entries of the condos.

"Not sure. We'll play it as it lies."

The front door was a shambles, smashed off its hinges and lying flat in the slate-floor entry hall. It was quiet inside.

"I'll go in," Calvin said, waving me back. Pistol in hand, he stepped around the remains of the door and edged silently along the hall. He passed a stairway leading up to the next floor, then continued toward a dining room-kitchen area.

I was unable to negotiate my chair past the flattened door, so I remained at the entrance and called 911. I then returned to the parking lot to keep an eye on the rear door in case Hackett tried to escape that way. Positioning my chair behind a three-foot-high boxwood hedge, I had a good view of the back of the house. I took a .22 pistol out of the tote sack and put it in my lap.

As I sat there in the dark I couldn't help but imagine what I could have done if I had the robot legs that I was waiting for. I'd be right in there with Calvin instead of sitting on the sideline, just waiting and watching.

Ten minutes later the rear door flew open and Hackett stepped out onto the stoop. Both his arms were behind him, as if he were handcuffed. Shoving him forward, Calvin then stepped out, his Glock jammed into Hackett's back. The siren in the distance was getting louder.

Calvin acknowledged my presence as I wheeled toward them, and then cuffed Hackett to a chain-link fence. "Carrie's not here. But there's some stuff I want to get. I'll be right back," he said, then turned and ran back into the house. A minute later he returned holding a black leather satchel which he immediately put in my van. He slid the door shut just as a police cruiser pulled up.

On the way back to my house Calvin filled me in on what had happened inside Carrie's. When he noticed a half-eaten plate of pasta and half-glass of red wine on the dining table, he concluded that Carrie either got Boyko's message and left in a hurry, or Hackett found her and had her upstairs. He then heard some noises coming from the upper level, and with pistol drawn, cautiously crept up the stairs. He discovered Hackett in one of the rooms shuffling through papers scattered around a desk, some strewn on the floor. Calvin easily got a drop on him, put on the plastic wrist ties and brought him outside to wait for the police. His assault on Boyko and this home invasion would be more than enough to put him back in prison.

"What's in the satchel?" I finally got to ask.

Calvin smiled. "Carrie's laptop, an address book and a day-planner. I knew you're curious about how she could afford such a high-priced house and what she's up to. Maybe you'll get some answers from this stuff."

Chapter Four

En route from Vancouver to Portland; Thursday, 1:20 a.m.

It didn't add up. Too many loose ends. Boyko had mentioned several times over the years that Carrie waited tables at a bar in Vancouver for minimum wage and tips. But the high-end condo, the expensive wines Calvin noticed in her wine rack, and the plush furniture and artwork screamed otherwise; Boyko claiming he knew nothing about her current situation, but finally revealing her address, and admitting he called her. I don't like unsolved puzzles, especially if it's one that I may have unwittingly created myself. It's not the money I spent on her legal defense ten years ago, but the possibility she used the new life my generosity allowed to launch some nefarious activity. Or that she had lied to me about her innocence. That she conned me into becoming her ally and patsy. And what about Hackett? Was there something compelling him to chase her down other than pure revenge? The more I thought about it, the more confusing the situation seemed, and the more anxious I was to fill in the pieces.

It was 1:45 a.m. when I pulled into my garage. I thanked Calvin, asked him to join Arvin and me for lunch the next day, and bid him goodnight. We were both spent from what we had been through, and there was nothing else we could do right then anyway. I grabbed the satchel that Calvin took from Carrie's condo and went to find Arvin. I knew he'd be awake; he never turned in until I returned from these late-night excursions.

"I was worried. Is everything alright?" Arvin asked when I found him in front of his computer.

I sat the satchel on his desk, then gave him a summary of what had transpired since we spoke when Calvin and I were on our way to Toby's Millhouse. Then I asked what he'd learned about Carrie.

"Dead ends on all fronts. It's as if she doesn't exist. The condo she lives in, in fact the entire triplex, is owned by a company with a Bulgarian post office box. There's no Oregon or Washington driver's license issued in her name. No telephone listings. Even Rantman came up with nothing. What's this?" he said, then pointing at the satchel.

"Her computer and address book. A day calendar, too. She must have bolted in a hurry if she left them behind. See what you can find. But now I'm heading to bed." I had to be up early in the morning for a regular day. "Would you please send Zachary to my room?" I said as I wheeled into the hall that led to my wing.

"Certainly. Good night, sir."

"Good night, Arvin."

Hawthorne Boulevard; Thursday, 8:46 a.m.

"Good morning, Mr. Samuelson," I greeted the elderly owner of the Happy Days tavern where Boyko had an evening bartending shift. I placed a half-dozen newspapers on the table inside the entrance and rolled up to the bar where Samuelson was checking stock and preparing to open at ten, then noticed three boxes of doughnuts stacked next to a large coffee urn. "Getting ready for the morning crowd, I see. Haven't seen you in a while. Is Johnny off today?"

"Johnny's taking Boyko's shift, so I'm doing this until I find someone to fill in for him. Boyko was beat up real bad last night and is gonna be out for a few weeks."

"Yes, I know. I saw him at the hospital last night. I wanted to find out where his cousin Carrie lives. Has Boyko ever mentioned her?"

"Don't remember anyone by that name. He's never said anything about a cousin. At least not one around here. He's only talked about relatives in Bulgaria. He even gets phone calls from there occasionally. Sometimes a couple of guys come in and they jabber away in Bulgarian. But no woman."

"Well, thanks anyway. Hope you find someone to fill in for Johnny soon." I spun around to leave, but hesitated, then turned back. "Those Bulgarian guys. How often do they show up?"

"Just about every week. Two of them. Always Friday afternoon. Boyko takes a break and has a beer with them. They sit together in one of the booths for ten minutes or so, then the two guys leave."

"What do they look like?"

"I don't know. Nothing special. Just regular guys. Maybe in their thirties, dark hair, one of them, a big guy, has a mustache. What's going on? Why the questions?"

"Just curious. I've known Boyko a long time. Thought maybe I'd know his friends, but I guess not," I said and started toward the entrance. "So long."

"Hey! You want a doughnut?" he yelled before I was through the door.

"No thanks. I'm still working off Chubb's bacon and eggs. See you tomorrow."

Portland; Thursday, 1:35 p.m.

Ginger put a pot of coffee on the sideboard and a plate of her macadamia nut cookies in the middle of the table.

"Thank you, Ginger. That chicken curry was fantastic," I said.

"Yes, I know."

"One of your mother's recipes, I suppose."

"No. One of Aunt Leela's. She was better cook than my mother, but stingy with her secrets. This one I had to force from her. It's no secret she wanted to marry my father, but lost him to her younger sister. She never forgave my mother. One time—"

"Yes. Well, thank you, Ginger, it really was a splendid lunch."

As Ginger headed back to her kitchen, mumbling in her native Malayalam language, I said to Arvin, "So. Find anything on Carrie's computer?"

"I couldn't get past her password. The tech guy at our law firm has it now. He said it should be possible to get into her files, but will take some time. He'll call as soon as he gets in. But there were some things of interest in the day planner besides hair and nail appointments. The name *Val* occurs frequently. And every four or five weeks there are what appeared to me to be airline flight numbers. When I matched the dates with the numbers, they turned out to be Delta arrivals in Seattle from New York, and Bulgaria Air flights into JFK from Bulgaria."

"Good work, Arvin. We'll make a detective out of you yet. Anything on the condo triplex?"

"No one's listed in any Vancouver city records as living in those other two units, but water and electricity are being consumed at considerable rates."

"What about Carrie's unit? Is she listed as the owner?"

"All three are owned by a post office box in Sofia. No listing for Carrie Hall in any record I could find anyplace."

"Okay. Calvin. Anything?"

Calvin took a little notebook from his shirt pocket and flipped it open. "I spent the morning staked out down the block from the triplex. At 7:35 this morning a guy wheeled a garbage bin from the rear to the front curb. At 9 a lawn maintenance guy arrived and mowed, did some edging and blew leaves and dust around with a blower. A little later two men arrived in a T&L Construction van and installed a new front door in Carrie's unit. But just before noon another man, a big guy with a mustache, parked at the curb and carried two bags up to the door of the middle unit. The bags looked like typical brown paper grocery sacks. After a minute the door opened and he entered. He came out six minutes later and left in his black late model Nissan Maxima. I left after he did to get here in time for lunch. I think I should return to see what else is going on there."

I then recounted what Samuelson had told me about Boyko's

two weekly visitors.

"Sounds like the guy I saw. There's gotta be a connection. There's too much tie-in with Bulgaria to be coincidental," Calvin observed.

"I agree. Is there a chance you could get back into Carrie's and do a more thorough search? You were in a big hurry last night and didn't have a chance to check everything out."

"Yeah, I know. I didn't want the cops to find me in there. I gotta make sure she hasn't returned, or that nobody else is in there. I'll give it a shot tonight. I want to know what's going on in the other two units, too."

"Good. I know you'll be careful. Just don't take any unnecessary risks."

"Arvin. Call the tech guy at the law firm and see how he's doing with Carrie's computer. The answers to this puzzle may be residing in her files, and if so, we need to access them sooner rather than later. In view of all the other item on our agenda, we need to close this case as soon as possible. By the way, is that *Val* name listed in her address book?"

Arvin reached for the book, opened it and slid it over to me. "The only name close is Valko Todorov. No address, just a phone number that matches codes for Sofia."

"Ah ha! The plot thickens. See if Rantman can get a lead on who this Todorov person is. He must have contacts in Europe that can dig up that kind of information. Anything else?" Arvin and Calvin both shook their heads.

Calvin took a last swig of coffee, scooted his chair away from the table, stood and said, "I'm heading back to Vancouver. I'll let you know if I find anything in Carrie's condo tonight."

"Okay. But call me when you're in position. I have a funny feeling about this. Keep in close contact."

"No problem," Calvin said as he started toward the front door.

"All right then, let's get on with it," I said as I followed Calvin out of the room with Arvin close behind.

"Arvin, would you ask Zachary to meet me in the gym? I'm

in desperate need of a workout. But before you do that, please get Betty on the phone for me. And bring up and chill another bottle of that Sauvignon Blanc we had with lunch. It really was quite nice." Halfway down the hall to the gym I stopped and looked back over my shoulder toward Arvin, who was still standing where I left him. "Are the people from the prosthesis company still coming tomorrow afternoon with the new prototype?"

"As far as I know, yes. At least they haven't canceled."

"Good."

Calvin went out the security gate set in the dense hedge, stood for a minute on the sidewalk and looked up and down the street. Seeing nothing out of the ordinary, he walked fifty paces north to where his car was parked, got in and started it. He pulled away from the curb and headed for I-5 North and back to his observation post across the river in Vancouver, anxious to solve the mystery of the elusive Carrie. But, even as sharp as he was, he failed to notice a blue sedan nose from behind a big delivery truck out into a flow of light traffic a half-block behind.

Chapter Five

Vancouver; Thursday, 3:15 p.m.

Calvin parked down the street from the condo triplex, laid his binoculars, camera and notebook on the seat next to him and settled in for what could be a long stakeout. In the rear-view mirror, he noticed a woman get out of a blue sedan several spaces behind and walk off. He recorded it in his notebook, but otherwise gave it little thought. The rest of the afternoon was uneventful, nothing to record other than mail delivery to each residence on the block except the triplex units.

Home, Portland; Thursday, 6:10 p.m.

A melodic chime announced Betty's arrival. Arvin glanced at the security camera screen, clicked the gate open, and met her at the front door. "Good evening, Miss Calvino. It's nice to see you again."

"Hello, Arvin. Yes, it's been a while," the tall raven-haired woman said, her smile reflecting genuine affection for the man ushering her in.

"He's in the library. Ginger said dinner will be ready around seven. I'll be in my office if you need anything."

"Thank you. Will you be joining us later?"

"I have a great deal of work tonight. But I'll see you before you leave."

"Good night, Arvin. See you in the morning."

Betty came into the book-lined oak-shelved library just as my phone rang. I glanced at the ID and waved Betty in. "It's Calvin. I better take it." As she passed my chair she playfully fondled my hair and kissed me on the cheek, then edged over to a little sofa.

Before answering, my eyes lingered a moment on two shapely well-muscled legs revealed after her short skirt slid up when she sat down. I caught myself staring, maybe a bit embarrassed, then pointed at the wine bucket with the loosely corked neck of a bottle sticking out. I quickly returned my attention to the phone.

"Calvin. Anything to report?"

"Nothing. Quiet as a morgue. It's gonna be dark in another hour. If no lights go on in Carrie's condo, I'll try to get in. I should be able to pick the lock on the new front door. I'll let you know what happens."

"Okay. But call me before you go in."

"You sure? I wouldn't want to interrupt anything between you two. I heard you say something to Arvin about Betty. Is she there?"

"No worry. We'll be eating dinner about then. Just call before you go in."

"Right. Tell her I said 'Hello.' Talk to you later."

When I ended the call, and returned my attention to Betty, who held out a glass to me, I couldn't help but notice the look of curiosity on her face.

"Sorry for the interruption. Calvin's on a case. But never mind that. How are you, my little butterfly?" I said accepting the wine and ignoring her apparent concern.

"Good! Big day at the clinic. A new staffer started this morning. Her specialty is shoulder and neck. That brings us to four full-time physical therapists. Now we have expertise from top to bottom, head to toes. Her coming on board means I can focus on what I do best; legs!"

I admired her enthusiasm and dedication. She and two colleagues had started a sports medicine clinic three years earlier and built it into a successful business. "That's great! I know you've been stressed out by not having enough coverage for upper body injuries after Hilda left. Here's to the new employee." We clinked our glasses and savored the perfectly chilled Sauvignon Blanc, one of the stars of my cellar.

"So, how did your judo meet in San Diego last weekend go?" I asked after a short pause, forcing my thoughts away from Calvin.

"More good news. I won six bouts! Even beat a fourth-degree black belt bruiser from Boise with a simple O-goshi, something she would never have expected from another black belt. It was my quickness that did it. Although those back flips are easier if you know your anatomy. But what surprised everybody was how I defeated a sixth-degree Korean with a Hadaka jime choke hold after a short mat grapple. Never under-estimate the effectiveness of a properly-placed choke-hold, especially when you go for a carotid instead of the trachea."

"Congratulations! I'll remember that advice," I replied, chuckling at the absurdity of ever having an opportunity to use such a technique. "But I did miss you. Four days away is four days too many."

"Yeah, sure. With all you've got going on I'd think you wouldn't even notice me being gone. You're too busy saving the world from evildoers, right? And helping people in trouble, right?"

"Well, I do what I can. How about a little more of that wine?" I asked, wanting to change the subject. The more Betty knew about my activities, the more danger she might be exposed to.

Before Betty could pour a second glass, the library door flew open and Ginger appeared, glaring at the two of us. "Dinner's ready. Don't let it get cold! Come! Now!"

"Okay. Okay. We're on our way. Betty, grab that bottle. It's too good to leave behind," I said as I wheeled toward the door and we followed Ginger down the hall. We were greeted by a table set for two, the only light from candles spread around the room. Soothing South India sitar ragas softened the lilac-scented ambience.

Home, Portland; Thursday, 7:25 p.m.

My phone rang as a spoonful of *crème* brûlée was halfway to my mouth. "It's Calvin. Better take it," I said, glancing at the phone next to my dish.

"Everything's still quiet here. No sign of life in Carrie's condo," Calvin reported. "I'm going in. I'll text you when I'm inside,"

"Be careful, and stay in touch." Although I knew Calvin was capable of handling himself and wouldn't do anything foolish, for some reason I had an uncomfortable feeling about what he was preparing to do.

"What's going on?" Betty asked. "You look worried."

"Calvin's checking into a situation across the river. Someone I helped a decade ago. She might be in trouble."

"Why do you do this? You and Calvin. And Arvin, too. Always helping someone in trouble. Inserting yourself into their lives."

I didn't think she was being critical, or even challenging. I sensed her sincerity from the tone of her voice and concern in her expression. "Because that's what we do. It's what I do. It's who I am."

"It's important, isn't it? It's what your life is all about," she replied after a moment, holding my gaze with her dark eyes.

I was quiet for a while, then said, "Yes. It *is* important. I inherited a huge fortune, and with Arvin's astute oversight increased it beyond all expectation. It's far more than meets my own needs. For some reason, not sure why, I feel obligated to use it to help others. Through philanthropy that Arvin and I oversee, but also in ways that are, I don't know ... personal, more ... involved. Maybe it's the excitement, the adrenaline rush. Maybe all those dreary years of inactivity when I was first struck with this damn polio have something to do with how I feel. Who knows? But I don't think I need psychiatric analysis to get to the root of some hypothetical addiction to danger, or other such nonsense. I just want to do some good, that's all."

To break the seriousness of the mood, I took that spoonful of *crème* brûlée, then another sip of wine.

"One more thing," I continued before Betty had a chance to respond. "Helping people in trouble isn't the only important thing in my life. You are, too. You must know that. Not only because you saved me from a sad existence of self-pity and isolation, but because of who you are. I couldn't bear the thought of losing you. I want you in my life."

"I feel the same way about you. But you *will* lose me if you continue to exclude me from such an important part of your being. Why would you assume I wouldn't feel like you do about people in trouble? Are you afraid I wouldn't be up to it?"

I was stunned by her statement, a reply that triggered thoughts of my parents willingly endangering themselves by remaining on the beach after rough-sea warnings. But as I started to explain that I only wanted to protect her from danger, she charged ahead, as if she were on the verge of an unavoidable declaration.

"So, here's the deal. I want in. To join you and Calvin. On the front line, so to speak."

"What? I can't let you do that. I won't put you in that situation. Too much risk. I won't chance losing you that way."

"If you want me to be in your life, it's gotta be all the way in. All the way, or no way. What's it gonna be?"

"Oh, my god!" I was having a hard time grasping her demand. I reached for the bottle, poured another glass and downed half of it in one gulp. "Do you know what you're asking?"

"Of course I do. I'm not stupid. I know there are lots of bad people out there. And that sometimes the cops need some help, even if they won't admit it. But I'm willing to take those risks. You do. Calvin does. I deserve that right, too. I hope you're not suggesting that because I'm a woman I'm too vulnerable."

"No. It's not that. It's just that—"

"Yes or no?" her voice was steady and unyielding.

I knew she meant business; her fierce determination was undeniable. I didn't want to lose her *this* way either, by denying her demand to join me in this pursuit of good versus evil. So, reluctantly, I consented. "All right. But only under certain conditions."

"No conditions. All in or all out. Your choice."

I gulped the rest of the wine, forced away the fears that clouded my mind, and reached across the table and took her hand. "You are a very stubborn woman. But since you put it that way, there *is* only one choice." I paused, searching for the right words, but failed; could only come up with, "Well, your life is about to change, honey. Maybe more than you could ever have imagined. Welcome to the party."

She grinned, squeezed my hand, then said, "I think it's bedtime already, don't you?"

"Indeed, I do." But then, as an afterthought, remembered Calvin in Vancouver and checked the time: 8:17, and no text or call from him.

"It's been a half hour since Calvin called. He should have gotten into Carrie's condo by now."

"Text him," Betty said, her mood instantly turning serious.

"What's happening? You okay?" I typed, then hit Send.

Ten minutes later, having received no response, I said, "He could be in trouble. I'll call the Vancouver police. And I need to get over there. Fast."

Without hesitation, Betty replied, "Call the cops while I change into something more appropriate. Then *we'll* head out. *Both* of us."

Chapter Six

En route from Portland to Vancouver; Thursday, 8:25 p.m.

I'd never seen Betty this anxious before. She's usually the epitome of calmness and self-control, but at that moment, on our way to Carrie's condo, she seemed apprehensive. "Was she changing her mind about what she earlier might have considered only a theoretical possibility of danger? Was she scared?" I wondered.

When we began my physical therapy six years earlier, and all through the following years of unrelenting effort, she never gave in to the difficulties we encountered. Not by the discouraging lack of progress at the start, or by the herculean effort required to stir the atrophied lower half of my body. Even my frequent tantrums didn't deter her. She was a rock. That I came to love her should be no surprise to anyone. Thankfully, she eventually reciprocated— I'd be lost without her. Knowing her strengths, I believed that she would be a reliable and valuable member of the team when I consented to her joining Calvin and me in our crime-fighting efforts. The first test was fast approaching. *Had my assessment been correct?* I wondered.

"We'll be there in ten minutes. The Vancouver police should be there soon, too. If Calvin's in trouble, we'll get him out of it," I said, as I shifted into the fast lane and accelerated.

Arvin called five minutes later. "The cops are no help. They did a drive-by and found nothing unusual. Checked the doors and looked around back. They can't do more, like break in, without a reason."

"Damn! If he's not answering his phone, *something's* wrong."

"What can we do?" Betty asked when I ended the call.

"We'll figure that out when we get there."

Carrie's condo; Thursday, 8:53 p.m.

I parked in a space half a block from the triplex. "Let's scope it out, like we're just strolling by," I said as we started toward the units.

"What should we be looking for?" Betty asked.

"Anything out of the ordinary." But nothing grabbed our attention in or near the three condos: no inside or outside lights, windows blocked by closed blinds or curtains, no sounds of music or TV. Same story around back, although there was a van parked there.

"We need to get in," I said, nodding at Carrie's condo as we paused by the hedge near the walkway to the rear entry.

"I'll try the door," Betty said. "Maybe Calvin got in and left it unlocked."

"If it's unlocked, don't go in. We'll go together." I took a snub-nose 32 revolver out of my tote bag. When she reached the door, she tried the handle, but without success, then peered through a nearby window. She looked at me and shook her head, then started back to where I was waiting.

That's when I noticed the sliding glass door on the second-floor balcony. It was partially open, an inch or so. Then I spotted a downspout running up the wall and passing close to the railing. A trash bin stood nearby.

"I bet that's how Calvin got in. Think you could climb up there?" I asked, pointing up at the balcony.

"Yes, if I stand on that bin."

"Once you're in, open the back door and we'll look around," I said, handing her the pistol. "Put this in your pocket. The safety's on so you'll have to—"

"Yeah, I know. Take it off if I have to use it. My dad taught me about guns."

I thought I noticed her tremble slightly as she took the gun, but dismissed it when she told me she'd have no problem getting up there and would be alert for any surprise. Promising to see me in a couple of minutes, she stuck the gun into her jacket pocket and walked away toward the rear of the condo.

I watched her climb to the balcony and scramble over the railing, as quietly as a skilled burglar. I was relieved when she slipped in. A minute later, a shadow fell across the glass panel of the back door, then it slowly eased open. When Betty appeared, and waved me forward, I wheeled up the walk. But instead of letting me in, she was suddenly shoved aside to reveal a man aiming a pistol at me.

"Get in here!" he yelled. "Now! You want I shoot girlfriend in gut?" he added when I hesitated. From his thick accent and his appearance, I assumed he was one of the Bulgarians that met with Carrie's cousin Boyko every Friday at the Happy Days bar.

"Okay. I'm coming," I said as I rolled past him. "We're looking for Carrie. We thought she might be in danger. I'm a friend of hers."

"Yeah? Was break-in guy friend, too? Why your girlfriend have gun? Not so friendly, I think," the man said.

"Where is he? What did you do to him?" I said, glancing around the kitchen.

"He is live, but does not talk. We try. Now you here, and this one," he waved the pistol at Betty, "I am thinking soon we get answers." He quickly moved behind me and reached toward the knob of the open door.

I had to do something, and do it fast. I needed to stop him from taking us to where Calvin was being held since there would likely be others there to contend with. I glanced at Betty, who had edged closer when the Bulgarian stepped behind me. She glanced at the Bulgarian, nodded at me and then shifted her stance.

When I saw the man reach for the knob, I wheeled backwards and rammed into him with all the force I could muster, knocking him off balance and out through the doorway. To our good fortune, his heel caught on the threshold and he tumbled onto his back. At the same instant, Betty dashed around my chair and kicked the pistol out of his grip. It spun through the air and landed in the grass alongside the walk. The man reacted with surprising speed and immediately started to get up, at the same time reaching into the pocket where he had put my pistol. But Betty was faster. She jumped beside him and threw her right arm around his neck, then reached around with her left arm and gripped her right bicep, allowing her to put incredible force into the same carotid chokehold that two days before had earned her a fourth-degree black belt. He tried desperately to fling her off as he rose and spun around, trying frantically with both hands to pull her arm away. But she hung on tenaciously until he collapsed a few seconds later. His Glock pistol lay on the lawn a few inches beyond his outstretched hand.

Betty quickly retrieved the snub-nose from the Bulgarian's pocket, picked the Glock up off the grass, then handed both to me in exchange for a roll of duct tape I took from my tote bag. "Do his legs, then his hands. I've got him covered."

The man stirred as Betty finished wrapping the tape around his ankles. He glanced around, then, like a striking snake, reached up and grabbed Betty by the hair and pulled her down to the grass and slammed his big fist into the side of her head. In the fraction of a second that I had a clear shot I took it, exploding a good portion of his shoulder with a single .32 round. He screamed and let go of Betty's hair. She rolled away and out of his reach, then stood and stumbled over to my chair.

"Move and I'll put one in *your* gut," I yelled over his unintelligible jumble of groans and Bulgarian raving. He must have heard me since he stayed down. Then to Betty, who had regained her balance, I said, "Call 911. Tell them to send an ambulance and the cops." When Betty finished the call, she ran to the kitchen, brought back a towel and threw it to the Bulgarian. "Slow the bleeding with this."

"Where's my friend?" I yelled.

"I say nothing," he growled through clenched teeth.

"Where is he?" I repeated.

"Fuck you!" he replied, pressing the towel to his blood-soaked jacket.

I aimed the pistol at his leg and pulled the trigger, intentionally missing him by a hair. "The next one will take out your knee. Where is he?"

"Don't shoot! He is in next house."

"How can we get there?" I said, rolling closer and pointing the pistol at his knee.

"Door inside. In hall," nodding toward Carrie's condo.

I glanced at Betty. "Tape his hands." I kept the gun pointed at his knee while she pulled his arms forward and wrapped the tape around his wrists, ignoring his cries of pain.

"All right. Let's go!" I shouted when she finished.

"Shouldn't we wait for the police?"

"Calvin's in trouble." I spun around and sped through the doorway into the hall leading to the rest of the condo. Betty was close behind. I heard the siren in the distance, but charged ahead anyway.

Chapter Seven

Vancouver; Thursday, 9:45 p.m.

With Betty close behind, I wheeled into the door that separated Carrie's unit from the one in the middle of the triplex. We paused when we reached it and listened for sounds from the other side. Hearing nothing, I cracked the door open a couple inches. Peering around the edge, I was greeted by total darkness.

"What do you see?" Betty asked.

"Nobody here. Let's go."

The dim light from Carrie's revealed another hallway with a door about ten feet straight ahead and another one nearer on our left. "We'll try this one," I said. Inside the narrow room we discovered after entering it, a bank of wall-mounted computer screens showed images of the areas surrounding the triplex.

"This is how they knew we were here. Probably Calvin, too. The guy you half choked to death must have been in here watching."

"This is sophisticated stuff. Wonder what they're protecting?" Betty asked, looking around at the computers and monitors and other gadgets.

"We're sure as hell going to find out. But first we have to find Calvin."

At that moment, the sirens went quiet and we heard car doors slamming.

"The cops are here," Betty said.

"We'll have to let them know what's going on. Especially about the guy we left out there," I said, spinning my chair toward the doorway.

Two cruisers were parked near the walkway, and an ambulance was just pulling up. Betty and I approached three cops who stood looking down at the Bulgarian Betty had subdued.

"Officers!" I said. "This man—"

"Who are you?" one of them demanded before I could finish. He was a captain and his name tag said "González."

"I know the woman who lives here. We came to check on her. The door was open, so we went in. This guy pulled a gun on us. There's no sign of the woman."

"You tape him up like this?"

"I did, officer," Betty said, stepping from behind my chair. "He was threatening us. But we managed to overpower him."

González gave Betty a skeptical look, then said, "What's going on?"

"Whatever it is, it's next door. He told us that my friend was being held captive and was beaten up. We've got to find him. You can get there through a door in here," I said, glancing at Carrie's condo. "We found a bunch of hi-tech surveillance equipment. Somebody's protecting something in there."

"Stay with him," González told one of the cops as two EMTs ran up to us and looked at the man on the ground. "You two wait here," he said to the techs. "Make sure that guy is okay, but don't undo his restraints."

"Show me this door," he then said to me.

González, the other patrolman, whose name tag said "Burt," and Betty followed as I wheeled through the condo.

"This is as far as we got before you showed up. We have no idea what's on the other side of the door at the end of *this* hall," I said to the captain before we entered the room with the monitors.

"You two stay here," González said after he looked around at the electronic equipment, then turned toward the door to the hall. "We'll see where that other door leads."

"Wait! Look at this!" Burt said, pointing at the monitor. "A woman and a man just ran out a door at the end of this building. See! . . . There, running across the grass," The couple then disappeared off screen, without any of us getting a view of their faces.

González took out his phone, put it on speaker and shouted to a cop in a squad car stationed out front, "Benson! A man and woman are running east on Garfield. I want them for questioning. No rough stuff!"

To Burt he said, "All right! Let's check out that door, see what the hell's going on here."

A minute later González's phone came to life: "There's no one around. They must have got away."

"Keep looking! They've got to be around there someplace," González yelled.

Meanwhile, González and Burt approached the door to the middle condo and paused to listen for sounds on the other side.

Without hesitating, I wheeled after them. "Come on," I said to Betty.

"They told us to stay here," she replied.

"Calvin must be in there!" I said, rolling out the door with Betty next to me.

When Captain González saw us, he said, "Hold on! You're—"

"We think our friend's in there. We're going with you," I said with more firmness than I had intended.

"All right, but stay behind. We'll go first," González said, drawing his pistol and motioning the other cop to open the door.

Another corridor greeted us, longer and wider than the one we were in. There was no one there, although bright ceiling lights were on and a rolling cart with packaged food on top was parked halfway down its length. There were solid doors spaced along both walls, a small glass window in each one.

"This looks like a prison," González said.

The other cop, who was checking out the cart, picked up a large ring of keys and started to say something when we heard what sounded like a feeble moan coming from the door nearest us.

"Burt! Open this door," González shouted.

"Oh, my god!" the cop said when he swung the door open. A young woman lay naked on a narrow wooden plank with a chain attached to a metal collar around her neck. The other end was fastened to a ring on the wall. Her hair was matted and she was filthy, covered in bruises and welts, whimpering like a terrified dog.

"Get those med techs!" González commanded Betty, then he yelled at Burt. "Open the other doors." He then called for more support. "We've got a situation. I need medical, CSI and more officers. It's bad. A hostage situation. Perps on the run."

I followed Burt as he unlocked the other doors, discovering another eight women, all in similar condition. Betty helped the two med techs look after the captives.

By the time we got to the last cell, I was worried we wouldn't find Calvin. I was afraid that maybe they'd killed him and taken his body away. "Hurry!" I said, as the cop fumbled with the key, "he has to be in here."

Finally, he got the door open. To my relief, there Calvin was, on the floor with his hands and feet shackled. He had tape across his mouth. He appeared to be unconscious, which judging from the blood, multiple cuts and massive swelling and bruising, must have been due to severe beatings.

"We need medical," I screamed at González, who was talking on his phone as he ran toward us.

"There's a crew on the way. Ambulances, too," he said, then told the cop to take the tape off Calvin's mouth.

Three hours, a score of EMTs, nine ambulances, and a dozen assorted other people later, Betty and I told González goodbye and we headed to Portland's Providence Hospital, where, at my request, Calvin had been taken.

En route from Vancouver to Portland; Friday; 1:25 a.m.

"We'll make sure Calvin's okay, then go back to my place," I said as we approached the Interstate Bridge over the Columbia.

"Good. I need some sleep. I have to work tomorrow . . . I mean today," Betty said, glancing at the dashboard clock.

"Me too. Have to keep up appearances. I want to check on

Boyko, anyway. The Vancouver police want us in tomorrow afternoon for an interview, and I want to know more about his involvement in this sex trafficking operation, if that's what it is."

The car phone rang as we were taking the Alberta Street exit. It was Arvin.

"You're still up?" I asked, before he had a chance to say anything.

"I just had a call from Rantman. And you're not going to like this. Hackett escaped this afternoon."

"What?"

"Three guys hijacked the prison van he was in, on the way from the Multnomah County jail to the state prison in Salem. One guard killed and another wounded. The operation was totally professional. There's no trace of Hackett."

With this news, I was rapidly approaching the end of my wits. But managing to pull it together, I said, "Arvin! Call Rantman! Tell him that Carrie escaped from her place in Vancouver tonight. At least I think it was her. She was with another man. Maybe one of her Bulgarian henchmen. Tell him about Hackett, too. Have him put out the word. I want these fuckers found. Goddamn it! This is really pissing me off!"

Somewhat calmed by my rant, I added, "We found Calvin. He's going to be all right. He's beat up pretty bad, though. We're on the way to the hospital, then we'll come home. Oh yeah, what's happening with Carrie's computer?"

"My guy couldn't get in to her files. He asked me if he could give it a friend who probably could. I said okay. I trust his judgement."

"Fine. Tell him I need whatever's in there by tomorrow. One more thing. Are the prosthesis guys still on for tomorrow afternoon?"

"Yes, sir. As far as I know. At least they haven't canceled yet."

"Reschedule. I have to be in Vancouver tomorrow. But only delay it one day. I want those robot legs! They would have come in handy today . . . We're here, have to go."

"Impressive. I've never seen this side of you. Certainly not that kind of language," Betty said, as we pulled into a lot near the ER entrance.

"Yeah. Well, sometimes I get riled up. Maybe a little over-zealous."

"I like it," Betty said. "Turns me on."

Chapter Eight

Portland; Friday, 7:45 a.m.

When I caught the bus that would take me to Hawthorne Boulevard and my newspaper delivery job, I had more than just newspapers on my mind. Foremost, being home for a four-o'clock robotic legs appointment. Calvin was also a priority, so the first thing I did after I rolled into a spot behind the driver was call the hospital.

Calvin answered on the third ring. "I don't look so good, but I'm gonna be fine. Nothing broken, no internal injuries, just a bunch of cuts and bruises. I'll get outta here tomorrow."

"Don't rush it. You were beat up pretty badly," I told him in no uncertain terms. "I'll try to stop by this evening or tomorrow morning. Maybe I'll have a surprise for you."

I also planned to confront Boyko, find Carrie, and put an end to the Bulgarian sex trafficking ring Betty and I had discovered in Vancouver the night before. I had a big day ahead of me.

I rolled into Chubb's restaurant 30 minutes later and wheeled to my regular table at the back. After Chubb took my order, I settled in to organizing my day, the first item being to locate Boyko. He was taking time off his bartending job at Happy Days tavern to recover from the beating Hackett gave him a few days before. Hopefully, his employer, Samuelson, would know Boyko's address since Arvin couldn't find it.

After Chubb took away the dishes and gave me a refill, I saw a young boy, maybe sixteen or seventeen, approach, but then halt several tables away and look at me as if he were waiting for me to call him forward. I smiled and waved him on, indicating an empty chair.

"Well?" I said after a moment.

"I heard you could help me find my mother and father," he said in a quiet voice.

He introduced himself as Alex in a thick Eastern European accent. He spoke hesitantly as he looked around the room. I jotted a few things in my note pad as he spoke, then told him to come back the next day.

"Where are you staying?" I asked as he rose to leave.

"I no have place. Sleep in park."

"That's no good. Meet me here at noon, we'll figure out something." There was something about the kid that caused me to make that decision, maybe the fear I detected in his voice, or the desperation of his situation.

I left a half-dozen newspapers for Chubb's, then headed west on Hawthorne, dropping off papers as I made my way toward Happy Days.

Samuelson was his usual pleasant self when I rolled through the door and stacked his papers on the entryway table.

"Good morning," I called out.

"Same to you!" he replied, opening a box of Crispy Cream doughnuts that sat next to a big coffee urn, his way of pulling in customers earlier than his competitors along the street. After the normal chit-chat, I asked him for Boyko's address.

"Isn't that confidential?" he asked.

"Yeah, I suppose it is. But I'm worried about a cousin of his who's an acquaintance of mine. I want to know if he's seen her lately."

"I'll call him."

I didn't like the way this was going, but didn't have much choice. "Okay."

After ten rings, Samuelson hung up. "No answer. No message machine, either."

"I'll be running some errands later, so I could stop by his place. I don't think he'll care if you give me the address." With a little more coaxing, Samuelson gave in and gave me the address of an older apartment building in Oregon City.

"If you see him, tell him I need him back on night shift as soon as he's able," Mr. Samuelson shouted, as I wheeled out.

I made it back to Chubb's at a quarter to twelve to find Alex waiting for me by the front door.

"Have you eaten anything?" I asked, noticing how gaunt he looked with his jacket unzipped and open.

"Papa has all our money."

"Come on! Let's go," I said, wheeling toward the bus stop. "We'll get lunch at my house."

Portland, Home; 1:10 p.m.

Arvin greeted us at the door, more excited than I'd seen him in a while.

"Arvin . . . Alex. Alex, this is Arvin. He makes sure everything in my life goes as smoothly as it can."

Alex looked at Arvin, then me, clearly having no idea what I meant by that.

"Alex will be staying with us for a few days. Ask Zachary to make sure the guest room is prepared. Maybe he could find some of my clothes that fit Alex. Seems that his family's possessions have disappeared along with his family."

"Of course, sir," Arvin replied, the confusion on his face changing to a brief smile before becoming serious again.

"Sir," Arvin continued, unable to stifle his enthusiasm, "the robot people will be here at four, and Miss Betty will arrive at six. And the hacker, I mean consultant, got into Carrie's files. What he discovered is most interesting!"

"That's great! You can tell me all about it after lunch! Tell Ginger we'll be ready in ten minutes. Now show Alex his room and I'll clean up."

Ginger was thrilled to have another mouth to feed, another person to appreciate her culinary genius, even though she would

Word Storms

never admit that she relished the compliments. Alex ate like a hungry bear, and Ginger gleefully grilled a second steak for him.

"What was in Carrie's files that's so interesting?" I asked Arvin when the table was cleared and fresh coffee poured. Alex sat in silence, but listened attentively.

Arvin retrieved and opened his laptop. "Look at this! Names and backgrounds for one hundred seventy-eight women. Photos, too. They're from all over Europe, some from Asia and Africa. What's more, it looks like the names of people who bought the women from Carrie are listed, and how much they paid. This is a goldmine for the police and the FBI. They'll be able to break up a major trafficking ring!"

"This is fantastic, Arvin. Good work! I'll give it to the Vancouver detective tomorrow when Betty and I meet with him. But they still have to find Carrie. By the way. Reward the *consultant* generously. Never know when we might need him again. Now, I'm going to the gym for a workout before the prosthesis squad arrives. Come on, Alex, I want to hear more about your parents and how you ended up in Portland."

Home gym; Friday, 4:05 p.m.

"Dr. Bellow is here, sir," Arvin announced as he led the prosthesis specialist and his engineer into the gym.

An hour later I was ready to try out the robotic aluminum-alloy appendages, a complex array of rods, pistons, hinges, and connectors that were strapped over my shriveled legs and wired into my nervous system. After so many failures in the past, I was apprehensive, even scared, but also guardedly optimistic. I had been waiting over a year for this moment, and desperately wanted it to be successful.

When Bellow said, "Stand up," I grabbed his outstretched hand.

I glanced down at the black, light-weight high-top boots,

attached at the end of the metal legs and firmly planted on the gym floor, then pushed myself up, holding Bellow's hand for support. I felt pressure on my lower trunk, but after a second, sensed a feeling of balance. At that moment, I knew I would be able to stay upright, and was overcome with a feeling of joy, of triumph, of unfettered optimism. "They feel good. They're going to work!" I cried out.

Still holding my hand, Bellow nodded, then said, "Take a step."

I had to think for a second about how to command my leg to move. It had been a long time since I had done that. I concentrated, and through some still-intact neuronal communication links, the metal leg miraculously obeyed. The boot moved forward and came to rest a foot or so ahead of the other one, and I still felt stable. Then I moved the other foot forward, released Bellow's hand, and stood unsupported on my own. I was ecstatic. "Thank you, Dr. Bellow. You've changed my life," I gushed.

I spent the next hour trying to learn to walk again, even trying a clumsy run halfway around the gym, maybe more of an awkward shuffle, but to me it felt like running. There was no pain, and the fit was comfortable. The long wait had been worth it. Before Bellow left, he showed me how to remove the legs, including disconnection of the nerve interface component, the most delicate part of the prosthesis system.

"Be careful with that connection. It's a prototype and hasn't been tested to the extent I would have liked. You were in a rush, so we incorporated it into this system without the usual field trials. Keep me informed about how it works," Bellow said as he and the engineer were leaving.

Betty arrived a few minutes later.

"Hello, my darling," I said as I walked up, paused a moment to stare at her at eye level, then took her into my arms.

"Oh, my God," she screamed. "You can walk!" Tears streamed down her cheeks, peals of laughter interspersed with sobs of joy.

That evening the entire household joined the "I can walk again" celebration. Ginger even abandoned her kitchen to eat in the dining room with us. Talk was lively, the beef bourguignon delicious and the champagne superb. Although two bottles of Dom Perignon were consumed, I limited my alcohol intake since I had plans for later that would require a clear head and steady nerves.

After the usual state of calm returned, I casually said to Betty, "Would you like to go for a ride? I'm anxious to see what it's like to drive with these legs."

"Are you sure? I thought you might want to make an early night of it, if you know what I mean."

"Right. But it's still early. We'll be back soon," I said, barely able to conceal my anxiousness to get going.

"How about Alex? Can he come along?"

"Sure. Why not?" I replied on my way out to the garage.

"Where are we going?" Betty asked when I headed south on I-205.

"Well, as long as we're out, I thought I'd drive by where Carrie's cousin Boyko lives. It's an apartment in Oregon City. You know, just check it out."

"What? You're taking us into another dangerous situation? After what we went through last night in Vancouver?" Betty said in an outburst so forceful that it caught me by surprise.

"I wouldn't do that. I just want to scope out the place, that's all. You can trust me."

She looked at Alex, who sat wide-eyed in the back seat. "Give a guy new legs and suddenly he goes all Batman on us," she said, her attempt at humor lost in the worry revealed in her voice.

"Come on, honey. I want to be prepared for our meeting with the Vancouver police tomorrow, that's all."

The lights were on in Boyko's ground-level apartment, but with the blinds closed we couldn't see inside. I parked half a block away and told Alex to stay in the van while Betty and I walked around a bit. On the way to Boyko's place, we noticed a blue sedan parked at the curb. Then it came to me: "That car was parked near Carrie's yesterday. I remember the dented fender."

"Maybe that's how the woman and man we saw on the surveillance monitor got away," Betty said.

"Yeah. They must have come here from Vancouver. She was probably unaware that I, or anyone else, knew Boyko was her cousin, and thought it would be a safe place to hide, at least until she got out of Portland. Let's check around back."

"Wait," Betty said. "Shouldn't we call the police?"

"Come on, we'll just take a quick look. If we see something suspicious, we'll call."

Betty followed as I started toward the end of the building, struggling along on my new legs, willing myself to ignore the slight clumsiness I felt.

A minute later, we stood behind an overflowing dumpster near a walkway that led to the rear entrance of Boyko's apartment. Light streamed through a window next to the door, but we couldn't see anything from where we were.

"I'll take a closer look," I said, as I stood and looked around to make sure the coast was clear.

"No! It's too dangerous!" Betty hissed. "Let's get outta here and call the cops."

"We will. First, I'm just gonna peek in the window."

I started along the walk, taking slow careful steps. Whether it was unwarranted confidence in my untested legs, or plain old hubris, that made me ignore Betty's plea at that point was irrelevant. The result was the same. Halfway along the walk the rear door flew open and a man, who must have been the other Bulgarian that Samuelson mentioned, burst out and rushed to where I stood and stuck a pistol in my face.

Determined not to be taken so easily, and reacting fast, I knocked the gun aside with a quick upswing of my left arm and unleashed an uppercut with my right that lifted the gunman an inch off the ground. Recovering faster than I expected, he stepped back and out of reach of my next swing, a left hook that found nothing but empty space.

Before he could throw a punch, I kicked out toward his crotch. But instead of landing what would have been a disabling blow, my other leg collapsed and I went down like a sack of wet sand.

Meanwhile, behind the dumpster, when Betty saw the man run out the door, she jumped up and dashed toward the confrontation. She reached the melee just as my robotic leg's nerve interface shorted out and the prosthesis gave way to the strain of my attempted kick. When the Bulgarian lunged for the pistol lying on the ground, Betty dove for it, snatched it up before he reached it, then did a shoulder roll into a standing position with the gun pointed at the man where he lay sprawled on the ground.

"Drop the gun!" a woman's voice said.

Betty turned to see a woman coming out of the apartment holding a pistol and swung her own pistol toward her.

"You must be Carrie," Betty said, breathing hard, but seemingly in control of her fury.

But as Betty turned away from the Bulgarian, he jumped up and rushed toward her. At that same moment, a form emerged from shadows along the back wall of the apartment and slammed into Carrie with such force that she crashed against the column supporting the overhang, dropped the pistol and collapsed with blood gushing from the side of her head. Simultaneously, Betty spun back to the big man rushing at her and fired a single shot. He cried out and fell into a nearby rosemary bush.

After Alex crashed into Carrie, he ran to me and straightened the twisted robot leg. "You okay?" he asked.

"Yeah. Just great! Find some rope or something in the apartment and secure that woman. Then get the Goddamn chair from the van," I said with as much disgust as I could muster. Then I noticed movement above me.

"Do you think we can call the cops now?" Betty asked, looking down at me where I lay helpless on the cold concrete walkway, a Glock in her right hand hanging at her side, a phone in her left, and an "I told you so" look on her face.

Hours later, in the van on our way home, I thanked Alex again for saving our bacon, as the saying goes, and told him we would do what we could to find his family. Betty was ecstatic that the sex trafficking ring had been destroyed, although distraught about having shot and seriously wounded her attacker. But me? As happy as I was with terminating Carrie's sex trafficking ring, I was devastated that the robot legs had failed. Would I ever walk again? Was that too much to ask?

At least we were able to rescue Boyko, who the police found tied up and gagged in the basement of his apartment, apparently until then unaware of the consequences of having given Carrie's henchmen the names of women in Bulgaria that sought legitimate employment in the US and Canada. Evidently, he had no idea what evil she and her mafia confederates had been up to.

"Tell Samuelson I'll be back at work tomorrow," Boyko had said, as we left his apartment.

"I will when I see him in the morning. I have to be at work, too," I replied.

"Me, too," Betty said. "You know, no rest for the . . . whatever."

"What about me?" Alex asked.

"Don't worry. We'll figure something out," I said, then. resorting to the van's manual controls. slipped into the fast lane and shot forward.

Gladstar Farm

There is a magical place called Gladstar Farm, where innocence and joy prevail. The narrator, Lillow Mi, is half Faeirie and half Witch, and her tales of Gladstar Farm, called taradiddles, or foolish tales, such as the one following, are of adventures she has with her friends the great Apes Ishmael and Ishytoo, the flying cow Holly Cow, Lorna Loon, and Meshach the Dragon. And now . . .

Raucous Offerings
By Silver Gladstar

I have crowed since I was young, learning the classic crows from the Red Roosters that lived around here. I have been innovative in creating new or interesting variations, and when Lorna Loon joined me for the morning Crow a couple of years ago, with her dulcet yet haunting calls, we became an amazing Crow team. And the Red Roosters know, as do Lorna and I, that it is crowing that brings the Sun back each day. I feel justified in saying that without us the world would end. Zippo gone! No Sun'd be bad! Real bad, like The End bad. So, we crow. And we dazzle and amaze with our style, élan and flair, all the while saving the Earth, day after day. Naturally, we were interested when we heard about the big Crow Off being held by the Red Roosters down at Mayday Ranch in Crater. I've never been to Mayday before, but Mom knows the head Witch there, Madeline Mayday, known as Maddy. Gosh, I think of our chef Taddy, and Grover Grosbeak's wife Gladdy: Maddy, Taddy and Gladdy! Imagine those three in the same room!

Woohoo! Anyway, Maddy Mayday has a daughter named Melody and Mom says she's a lot like me! Except she doesn't crow.

Lorna and I got registered in the Crow Off so now we're practicing and practicing! We'll go with a polished performance! I arrive at the upper perch on the manor as the sky in the east is growing lighter. I hear Lorna arrive but don't look at her as I stare intently at the brightening horizon.

"Morning, Lorna." I say, staring east.

"Morning, Lillow." she says, also staring east. We're silent as we gaze, and I feel the intensity of the situation, the horizon getting brighter, our nerves getting taut. Then the first golden rays appear as Father Sun peeks over to see if he should continue. I let out a traditional Red Rooster crow as Lorna accompanies with a haunting phrase ending in undulating ululations while I tremolo. We finale with a harmonic vibrato. Father Sun is pleased and he advances. I break into the Rooster song of appreciation and gratitude while Lorna sings the Loon song of joy. Then we encourage and love Father Sun with a crow of our own devising, blending parts of the traditional Rooster with Loon and Parakeet renderings. It is sublime, and we strut in circles flapping our wings. Father Sun continues to advance, and we turn jubilant and do the Blessing Crow: a fine full-bodied crow with Loony endearments and brilliant harmonies. Father Sun clears the horizon, smiling down on us, and we celebrate! Another day! Now we dance in circles around each other and begin the crow of loving acceptance and appreciation. Many of the local fauna have joined us by now, and our finish is orchestral. We lie down panting when it is done, and after sufficient rest we make our way to the main hall for breakfast. As I turn to go, I see Ishmael and Ishytoo walking up the trail by Holly's Palatial Estate, returning from the Shine. They're chattering and laughing and I wave. Ishytoo sees me first and waves back, then Ishmael waves. The day is begun!

Ishmael and Holly Cow are going with us to Mayday Ranch, and we'll go the day before the Crow Off. Ishmael is to be our manager and Holly is our press secretary. Sounded pretty hifalutin to me, but they both were so eager and wanting to be a part that we agreed.

What could it hurt? Meshach will come down the day of the performance, and he'll bring Ishytoo and any of the Elves who want to come. Jack Ass will be there, and the Witches, along with Nonesuch, Taddy and Hayu, will come by broom. Excitement builds!

Grover Grosbeak came by and told me he was taking the family to watch.

"That's marvelous, Grover!" I say. "Gosh! The little ones are big enough to travel?"

"We think so. Gladdy is so proud of them, watching them fly around the nest. But I swear she thinks they could fly the whole way themselves!" and he laughs. "But I nixed that idea real quick! Meshach's taking us all together. We don't take up much space after all."

I laugh, "I don't expect so! But I'm sure glad you're coming! Home town support, you know?"

He laughs, "Yeah. We'll be rooting for you! I know you'll win, but I hear there's some pretty stiff competition."

"What'd you hear?"

"I heard that Red Marvel, the regional champ, is coming down from Elvenstead."

"Oh yeah?" I hadn't heard that, but I remained nonchalant. Darn! Red Marvel is good!

"Yeah, and I heard Sterling Hicall and Morning Glory Rooster were both competing this year."

I'd heard of Morning Glory and I was shaken but still not showing it. Pretty sure. Sterling Hicall has been around a while, practically a legend, but not serious competition anymore. Pretty sure.

"And then there's Ruggy Rooster, Mayday's champion."

I knew of this one and I was pretty sure we could beat him.

"And then there's all these new guys looking to make a name . . ."

"Well, Grover, I think we're in pretty good shape, you know? I think we'll be just fine."

"Oh yes! I know it! I fully expect you and Lorna to take it!"

I gave him a thumbs up as I walked away. Darn! Red Marvel!

Morning Glory Rooster! Darn!

After I told Lorna what I had heard, we both fretted for a while. Then Lorna said, "You know, Lillow, this is our first time competing. We've only been together, what? A year and a half?" I nodded yes, "And we really don't know what we're facing, so let's just go and do the best we can!"

I nodded glumly. She was right, of course. Worrying doesn't fix a thing. All we can do is do our best! "So how about a little practice?" I asked.

Lorna smiled and began the low warble of a particularly difficult passage in our Morning Song Crow and I joined in. We did marvelously well!

Later in the meadow, Holly came rushing up to me, "Oh, my heavens, Lillow! Did you hear? Red Marvel! Oh, my heavens! He'll be there! Red Marvel! Competing! Against you! And Lorna!"

"Holly, calm down. We already know. It's fine, okay?"

She looked at me with big sad cow eyes. "Yeah, sure, Lillow. You'll be fine."

Dang! I sure haven't had a lot of confidence-building experiences lately.

We left for Crater early the morning before the competition. It's about a half day's flight from the farm and we set off with high spirits! Lorna rode on Holly's back and Ishmael and I took brooms. Mayday Ranch sits inside a giant crater and shares that space with a lake and an island called Shadow. Across the lake near the bottom of the crater wall is an opening, and there are deep rumblings and dark red glowing lights from within. It is called the Gate to Hek and is similar to our own Swamp of Doom. Mom says magical places tend to have dark spots like that. It's sort of a balance for the magic, she says, like poles. The magic, which is in itself the purest good, is offset by something dark. There is a mad old woman that lives in the Gate named Hoggan, and they think she's probably a Witch and likely at least a hundred years old! Fortunately, she's almost never seen, and the residents know better than to go in there. Like the swamp, it has a warning sign saying 'abandon ye all hope who enter here'.

There is a road that is carved out of the crater wall that goes to the top. It circles one complete time around the crater and emerges at the rim at the precise spot where it starts in the bottom. But we fly in, bypassing the road entirely, and land in the clearing in front of the main building. Reminds me of Glad Manor in some ways and is clearly the center and most important part of the ranch. As soon as we touch down, a Witch comes running out followed by a couple more Witches and an Elf, and they head toward us. "Lillow and Lorna?" she asks when she arrives.

"Yes," I answer.

"Well, I'm glad to meet you! I'm Madeline Mayday, but you can call me Maddy, and this here's Zanilly Dunn the Witch of the North, and Trudy Wundir the Witch of the East, and our good friend Elfbliss Enderly," pointing to each as she named them and they each nod and offer a how do you do or the like in turn.

"I'm pleased to meet you! I'm Lillow Mi and this is my partner Lorna Loon and our manager Ishmael and our press secretary Holly Cow." I think she was impressed by those titles. I hope so, anyway. They gave us rooms in the Bunkhouse which was a large long building next to the ranch house, which was called Castle Mayday, or just the castle. I noticed some roosters standing in the shadows watching us as we went in.

Soon after getting settled, we had lunch in the castle, followed by a tour of the ranch, led by the Witch of the south, Sunny Vale, and the Witch of the north, Zanilly Dunn, who we met when we landed. They had a wagon that was magically driven, like the bussels in Elvenstead, by an old Elf named Pally Elfmor. We all climbed on board and away we went! I learned from Sunny, who was animated and chatty, that the wagon we were in was called a waggel, and, like the bussels in Elvenstead, was magically controlled by the spells of the driver. Gosh, I thought, this's what we need on the farm. Zanilly was more taciturn by nature than Sunny, but interjected useful bits of information from time to time. The first place we went to was the range, which was like the meadow back on the farm. We'd heard there was a band of long little doggies that roamed here, but we didn't see them at first.

A large oxen-like creature walked up to us as we sat in the waggel viewing the range. Smiling, he introduced himself. "Hey, you all! Haven't seen you before! I'm Buffalo Rome! Welcome to my range!" I introduced myself and my cohorts. He already knew the Witches.

"Gosh, Buffalo."

"You can call me Buff!"

"Gosh, Buff," I continued, "your range is beautiful!"

"Thank you, thank you!" he said, obviously pleased. "Lotta work in a good range, you know."

It looked a little like the high plain desert we camped on going to Mish, that is, a natural untended place, but I didn't say anything.

"C'mon and meet the long little doggies!" he said and set off across the range. We followed in the waggel. From time to time Pally would name an interesting plant or tree as we passed. We soon came to a small grove of trees and I could see a little pond in the center as Buff called out, "Hello! Doggies! Hello!"

Five long brown dogs with madly wagging tails came running out from the grove, grinning and barking.

"Hey, Doggies," he said, "calm down! I want you to meet our guests," and he introduced us to Werner, Landorf, Alois, Getta and Horacio Long Doggie, who gathered around us wagging and barking. They reminded me of the Prairie Dogs in Thippen. We ran and fetched and had a wonderful time! Bidding a fond farewell to Buff and the Doggies, we boarded the waggel and moved towards the lake.

We arrived at a series of docks on the lake, which is called Lake Crater, and each dock had a boat. We left Pally and the waggel and boarded a boat that took us to Shadow Island. The island was on the extreme southern part of the lake and was in shadow even though it was early afternoon. This part of the lake gets maybe an hour at best of sunlight, and that just on the summer Solstice, before it's shaded again because of it being so close to the southern wall. But the island was beautiful and fully suited to its shadowy existence. There is a lodge on the island for people to use when they're there and we head for that.

We are greeted by an elderly Elf couple who introduced themselves as the hosts of Shadow House, Elwood and Elsia Elvengold. They led us to a dining room in the rear of the house where they served us tea and biscuits. Through the large picture window, we could see a narrow expanse of lake and the crater wall just beyond. Right in the middle of our view is a black red-glowing hole, or maybe a doorway with no door. It was hard to tell anything in that gloom.

"The Gate to Hek," said Elwood solemnly, standing by the window. As we looked, some lightning flashes crackled out of the entrance of the gate with loud cracks that made us all jump. Well, all except Elwood and Elsia, who seemed unaffected. "The home of Witch Hoggan and her dark minions," Elwood intoned in dark tones.

"Somebody lives in there?" asked Ishmael, who was visibly shaken by the thunder.

"As far as we know," answered Elsia as she brought a tray of cookies to the table. Everyone began chattering at once, nervous energy I think, but I continued to look at the gate. As I looked, a dark figure emerged and stood looking at me. I looked around to see if anyone else saw it, but no one was looking as they continued their animated discussion, and when I looked back it was gone. I had a feeling it was female, but I couldn't be sure, and I thought of the dark Witch Hoggan said to dwell inside the gate. This was the closest I wanted to get to that gate, that's for sure.

Pally dropped us off at the Mayday Castle and we went to the bunkhouse to freshen up. Lorna and I shared a room, but Holly and Ishmael each had their own space. It reminded me of Holly's Palatial Estate. We went for supper in the main hall at the Castle and I sat with Ishmael and a couple of Witches and two Elves. Lorna and Holly sat with some surly looking Roosters, but were separated from them by an Elf. They seemed fine though, so I didn't worry. Our table was a fascinating group; Sunny Vale, Witch of the south, who we had met already, and Clare Water, Witch of the west, were the Witches, and Jilly Elvengold, daughter of Elwood and Elsia of Shadow Island, and Elvin Brightsky were the Elves.

"Yep, I'm their daughter," said Jilly when I commented on her last name being the same as theirs.

"We had a good time on Shadow Island," said Ishmael. "They're good hosts."

"Too gloomy for me!" said Jilly, "I was glad to leave when I came of age, but I still go out to visit them a lot. They rarely leave the Island." She paused, looking sad. "Did you notice how pale they were?"

"No, I didn't really," I said as Ishmael nodded no. "But who can tell in the gloom, huh?"

"It's their proper environment, I guess," Jilly sighed. "But I live in the Sun!"

"Good for you, Jilly!" said Sunny. "Your folks are good people, but I agree! You need sunlight!"

"It was sure scary seeing the Gate to Hek," I said. "Did it bother you growing up so close to it?"

"I didn't like it, but no," she answered. "I don't think it did. I never looked at it much. My room was in the front of the house where I couldn't see it out my window, and I came to school over here at Mayday, so it wasn't a big part of my life."

"Scared me," said Ishmael.

"Does a Witch really live in there?" I asked.

"I've met her," said Clare. We looked at her round-eyed. "It was many years ago when I first joined the Mayday Coven." She paused, looking off. "Gosh, that's hmmm, 27, no, 28 years ago now!" Then she smiled at us.

"Time flies," said Sunny, who I know had heard this story before.

"Deed it does!" she continued. "So, let's see, I had just attained my Adept status and had joined a new coven and I was feeling cocky." She smiled ruefully, "So I up and walked around the crater wall on the southern lake shore until I reached the gate." She paused, chewing on some food. "So, I just stood there looking at it!

I had no plan, and frankly it was really starting to creep me out."

"It creeped me out just seeing it from the lodge on the island," I said.

"It's creepier up close," she continued. "Well, I was just about to turn around and come back when this dark figure appeared in the gate."

I'd seen a dark figure! But I didn't say anything. "As I watched," she continued, "it floated down toward me. I was terrified but I couldn't move! Like I was cemented to the spot. When she got close I could see the haggard face of an old, old woman under her hood."

"Welcome to Crater, Clare of the Waters," the old woman said. I was shocked but managed a lame thank you. How could she know my name? I could hear her chuckling. "You're frightened? Well, perhaps you ought. It was brave of you to come here."

I finally managed to speak, "Uh, thank you. I, uh, I think I ought to get back now. They'll miss me."

"Hek is where the dark things go," she said in a droning tone, ignoring my statement. "I see them pass me all the time. Going fast by the time they are once in the gate and always going in." She paused and stared right at me, her demeanor fierce, her eyes penetrating. "Never out!" We all shivered and I could feel goose bumps. "Right then my feet came loose and I turned and ran! I ran until I was too winded to run and had to stop and catch my breath. Looking back, I could see the gate in the distance, but no sign of the old woman."

"Witch Hoggan," said Sunny confidently.

"I expect," said Clare, smiling. "But I've never gone back to make sure."

"Maddy's seen her," said Sunny, "and," looking at Jilly, "so has your mom."

Jilly nodded. "I know, but she never talks about it."

"I saw a dark figure this afternoon when we were at the lodge on Shadow Island," I said. "Standing right in the gate looking at me, but I don't think anyone else saw it." I looked at Ishmael.

"I didn't," he said. "And no one else mentioned seeing anything odd."

"Wow, that's pretty impressive," said Sunny as Clare smiled at me.

"You're an Adept, are you not, Lillow?" asked Clare.

"Well, that's what they told me. I don't feel any different, but the Tomes do talk to me."

"Yes. That's a sign. And you saw Hoggan?" she continued, looking at me intently.

"Well, I saw a dark figure. Looked female, but I couldn't really tell. She looked right at me and then she was gone."

Sunny and Clare exchanged enigmatic looks, and Sunny continued, "Well, that's something. Not sure what, but it is something," with Clare nodding agreement.

The next morning all of us contestants were lined up on a platform on top of the Bunkhouse. We were all going to crow at the same time, when the Sun came up, and the judges were to rove back and forth in the crowd below us. I could see the crowd fairly well in the predawn light, but my attention was drawn to the eastern horizon, in this case the top of the crater wall, and I stared, transfixed, as did my fellow crowers, as the sky slowly got brighter. We were all tense near to breaking when the first rosy streamers appeared with the hint of Father Sun peeking over, looking to see should he continue. And we all cut loose! What an amazing cacophony! I think Father Sun faltered and I slipped into my encouraging gratitude song and I heard Lorna easily follow and quickly embellish. And others did likewise and Father Sun presented more of his face.

We were all so excited, and we fed off of each other's energy until we were all strutting and flapping our wings and cawing to our hearts' delight! I could hear the crowd cheering and applauding after many of the crows. They applauded several times in front of me and Lorna, but our attention was to the sky! And Father Sun, amazed at this spectacle, showed more of his face, watching us. And we became louder, more animated, dancing and stomping, as our calls and screeches echoed off the crater walls. I heard a loud creaking noise and I felt our platform wobble, so I stood on my toes to ignore this distraction as did most of the others, flapping and cawing. Reaching new heights and stomping our feet while dancing on our toes, we suddenly heard another screeching noise and the platform gave out from under us and we all went sliding off the roof!

The crowd pushed back as we fell and they mostly got out of the way but I did bump into Holly. We'd all instinctively spread our wings as we cleared the roof so we landed soft but there was confusion and mayhem everywhere, along with the pieces of the platform. Ishmael came running up to see if we were okay and I looked at Lorna who smiled back and I assured him we were fine. Only our pride is damaged as we lay there looking up at Father Sun showing his full face and clearly laughing!

Later we learned that the stage, which was re-erected each fall for the Crow Off, had broken loose because of two things: more contestants than ever before and the contestants were much more lively, you could even say raucous. Maddy said the Crow Off this year was much more energetic than any she'd seen before! And she's born and raised Mayday.

"Why, you crowd of crowers made a bigger ruckus this year than I'd even thought possible!" she exclaimed. "My ears are still ringing!"

"Never saw 'em caw the roof off before!" said Sunny grinning at us.

I didn't know whether that was good or bad, and I think we were all squirming a little.

"Clearly, you were all fabulous!" Maddy continued, grinning broadly. Then she quickly frowned, "But I'm afraid the judges were unable to determine a winner."

"Couple of judges flew the coop!" said Sunny, smiling brightly.

"Yes, well, be that as it may, we have no decisions." Groaning erupted from the crowd. Then she was smiling brightly again, "So we're going to declare a tie! That's right! You're all tied for first place!" And she started clapping loudly with Sunny joining in. Then she started walking amongst us passing out blue ribbons saying, "Good job! Well done! Splendid!" things like that.

Sunny followed behind, shaking our hands muttering, "Congratulations," over and over while smiling brightly.

There was a smattering of applause and some discontented grumbling, but we all accepted our tenuous winning status. We could see no other way.

After a quick breakfast, we left, returning to the farm. They invited us back next year, but we aren't real sure we want to go. We'll see. Lorna and I each got a blue ribbon and we hung these in the main hall for all to see. Mom engraved a plaque with our names under the heading, "Winners!" and placed it above the blue ribbons. I looked on, unsure of my feelings, and thought of the Witch, Hoggan. Well, at least we didn't lose. Pretty sure.

THE END

Acknowledgements

We would like to thank Jill Powell, Raina Glazener, Keith Buckley and Kerry McPherson for their invaluable assistance in making this book possible.